Henry Cecil was the pseudonym of Judge Henry Cecil Leon. He was born in Norwood Green Rectory, near London, England in 1902. He studied at Cambridge where he edited an undergraduate magazine and wrote a Footlights May Week production. Called to the bar in 1923, he served with the British Army during the Second World War. While in the Middle East with his battalion he used to entertain the troops with a serial story each evening. This formed the basis of his first book, *Full Circle*. He was appointed a County Court Judge in 1949 and held that position until 1967. The law and the circumstances which surround it were the source of his many novels, plays, and short stories. His books are works of great comic genius with unpredictable twists of plot which highlight the often absurd workings of the English legal system. He died in 1976.

GW00642554

PORTRAIT OF A JUDGE

AND OTHER STORIES

by

Henry Cecil

HOUSE OF
STRATUS

This edition published in 2000 by House of Stratus, an imprint of
Stratus Books Ltd., Lisandra House, Fore Street,
Looe, Cornwall, PL13 1AD, U.K.

www.houseofstratus.com

Printed and bound by CPI Group (UK) Ltd, Croydon, CR0 4YY

A catalogue record for this book is available from the British Library
and the Library of Congress.

ISBN 1-84232-062-9

Contents

Portrait of a Judge

The gales of the last few days had abated, and Mr Justice Pantin was sitting, as happily as his gout would allow him, in the garden of his little cottage. He was the oldest Queen's Bench judge, and those who knew him realised that he would never retire. Since his wife's death many years before, he had lived by himself in a flat in London, but he spent his weekends and most of the vacations in his country cottage, looked after by his old housekeeper Mary.

He was well known to the public, partly by reason of the apparent severity of some of his sentences but also for the fairness of his decisions and the coldly logical manner in which he approached every case, no matter how great the human interest.

If you came before him on a criminal charge and were innocent you could not wish for a better judge. You were certain to be acquitted. If, however, you were guilty but had emotional or sentimental reasons for the crime you had committed, you could feel quite sure that such reasons would not appeal to the judge. He tried each case with calculated methodical precision and, indeed, as far as one could tell, he conducted his life in the same way. It is difficult to think that, if he had been standing in the dock himself instead of sitting on the Bench, he would have asked for more mercy from his judge than he, as a judge, was prepared to give to the offender. On one occasion a prisoner convicted of a serious crime was suffering from a deadly disease and, on being sentenced to three years' imprisonment, informed the judge that he would die in prison. 'You should have thought of that before,' Mr Justice Pantin had said.

The judge was eighty-four years old. Sixty-four years before, he had won the quarter-mile and put the weight for Cambridge, but he was now crippled with gout in both feet. He sat in a deckchair, with his books on one side and sandwiches and a vacuum flask on the other. It was a lovely day, and he was looking forward to making the most of it, partly in reading and partly in meditation.

He was self-sufficient and enjoyed his own company. Mary had been given a day off to go to see some friends in London, but she had made certain before going that everything was provided to make him comfortable. And, apart from his gout, he was very comfortable, sitting in the warm sunlight and pleased with the thought of a whole day with himself and his books.

He had just finished an article in the *Law Quarterly* on a technical aspect of the criminal law when a stranger came into the garden.

'What d'you want?' said the judge.

'To talk to you,' replied the stranger. His voice was cultured, soft and confident. He was small and light-framed and might have been described as puny, but for the air of menace about him.

'I don't think I know you,' said the judge. 'Who are you?'

'I doubt whether my name would mean anything to you,' said the man, 'because, at the moment, it is "Smith".'

'You had better go then,' said the judge.

'I shall do nothing of the kind,' said the man. 'I shall stay here until I have finished what I have come to do. I'm afraid this is one of those rare occasions – possibly it is the only occasion – when someone is in the position to dictate to you.'

'Will you kindly go away?' said the judge.

'I will reconsider your request,' said the man, 'if you will tell me what you will do if I don't.'

It did not take Mr Justice Pantin many seconds to realise that there was nothing he could do. His housekeeper was out; his telephone was out of order; he was quite unable to walk three-quarters of a mile to his nearest neighbour and, unless someone else happened to visit him, which was unlikely, he would have to endure the presence of the stranger until he chose to take himself off.

'I order you to leave my garden,' said the judge. 'Unfortunately I cannot compel you by force to do so and, if you refuse to go, I can only wait until someone else arrives here.'

'Precisely,' said the man, 'and, if the results of my inquiries are not wrong, that cannot be for some time. Accordingly, I propose to talk to you.'

'I don't,' said the judge, 'propose to talk to you.'

'That may be,' said the man, 'but I think you will do so none the less. Forgive me a moment. I can talk more easily sitting down. I will go and get a chair.'

He went into the cottage, returning shortly with a chair, which he placed in front of the judge. The latter had in the meantime picked up a book and started to read.

'You can pretend not to listen as much as you like, but you will find it physically impossible not to do so. So you might as well hear what I have to say with a good grace.'

The judge made no answer.

'Some years ago,' said the man, 'you sentenced a friend of mine to death. If it had not been for your summing-up, my friend would probably have been acquitted. At least, that is what most people thought. As it was, you were so convinced in your own mind of his guilt that you gave him no chance. One of my reasons for coming here is to show you how wrong you were, though I don't imagine that that will have much effect upon the parchment which serves you for a mind.'

Although the judge could not in fact help hearing what was being said, he gave no indication that he had done so.

'You are so cocksure of your own infallibility,' went on the man, 'that I imagine that nothing can shake you. Let me see whether this makes any difference. I, in fact, committed the murder for which Frank Turner was hanged.'

The judge remembered Turner's case, but still gave no sign that he was listening. Nevertheless, he could not refrain from casting his mind back to the trial and trying to recollect what was the evidence.

He was not in the least concerned with the man's statement. Frank Turner had been tried according to law and had been found guilty. He had appealed to the Court of Criminal Appeal and his appeal had been dismissed. If he were innocent fifty times over, it could make no difference now, nor was the judge much concerned with his innocence or guilt. Laws made by human beings are fallible and, occasionally, an innocent man may be found guilty. The judge's only duty was to see that the law was duly applied. If, after a proper trial, with proper evidence and a proper summing-up, the jury returned a verdict of guilty, that was an end of the matter. If the man happened to be innocent, that was either the fault of the jury or due

4

to the inevitable fallibility of any legal system made by man.

'I suppose you wonder why I am telling this to you, but you cannot hang me as well, can you?'

The judge was unable to resist replying that the stranger could certainly be hanged.

'What, both of us?'

'Certainly,' said the judge.

'D'you mean to say that, if a crime is committed by one person only, you can hang one man for that crime and subsequently hang another?'

'Half a dozen, if necessary,' said the judge.

'Oh, well,' said the man. 'Never mind. You won't hang me.'

'I think,' said the judge, 'the man who was hanged for your crime, as you call it, was your friend?'

'That's right.'

'Then why did you not come forward in time?'

'Well, since you ask me, in the first place I had a great faith in English law and I didn't believe it possible that a man could be convicted of a grave crime of which he was innocent. Secondly, I must admit that I was not prepared to sacrifice my life, if the law went wrong.'

During this conversation, the judge had recalled some of the circumstances of the case and he did remember, with a slight shock, that the defence of the prisoner had been an alibi.

'What is the purpose of your visit?' asked the judge.

'I'm glad I have interested you,' said the man. 'In the first place, it is to try and lower your own self-esteem. Have I succeeded at all in that?'

'You have merely succeeded in being insolent,' said the judge, 'and you are well aware that, if it were not for my age and physical infirmity, you would not have had the opportunity.'

'Nevertheless,' said the stranger, 'I have the opportunity and propose to take it. Would you like to know how, when and why I murdered Mrs Blazegrove, so that you can satisfy yourself that you were a party to sending an innocent man to his death?'

'Not in the least,' said the judge. 'If you have any statement to make, it should be made to the police. I have nothing further to say to you.'

'Very well,' said the stranger. 'You have behaved much as I expected, and I suppose I must now pass to the second object of my visit. This is simply stated – to kill you.'

The judge made no reply.

'I think,' said the man, 'this will be unique in judicial history. I expect you have received threatening letters in your time, but, so far as I know, no one has yet even assaulted a judge, let alone killed him. I don't, of course, count the case of the man who threw tomatoes at the Court of Appeal. In any event he missed.'

As the judge still remained silent, he added: 'There is no good in your pretending to ignore everything that is going on, because very shortly you will have to take a part in the operation. I should like to explain it to you before it begins. Then, perhaps, you can tell me what are my chances of avoiding a conviction. I will tell you what I am going to do. I am going to get the shotgun at present in your cottage, and I am going to kill you with it.'

He paused, to let the words sink in. The judge said nothing.

'If I just killed you with it and ran away, it is conceivable that someone could identify me as having walked along this road, and it is possible that I should eventually be caught and hanged. It would be obvious that you had been murdered and the only question would be who had done it. I don't propose to take this risk. I propose to hand you your shotgun and to see that it goes off in a struggle when it happens to be pointed at you. I shall then immediately go for help and, at the earliest possible moment, I shall inform the police who I am and, to some extent, why I came here. I mean by that that I shall tell them that Frank Turner was my friend, that I believed him to be innocent and that I came to give you a piece of my mind. I will then say that you ordered me off the premises and that, when I refused to go, you produced your shotgun to reinforce your order.

'I shall add that, being frightened that you might be going to fire, I tried to take it from you and that, unfortunately, in the struggle it went off. Now, assuming that I tell that voluntarily to the police as soon as possible, do you consider that there is any chance whatever of my being convicted of murder?'

The judge, realising that the stranger might mean what he was saying, decided that he had better take a more lively interest in the proceedings.

'If the medical evidence were consistent with your story, I doubt whether you would be convicted of murder,' he said. 'There is a possibility that, having regard to my age and infirmity, a verdict of manslaughter might be returned, but that would depend upon the whole of the evidence. Probably you would be acquitted altogether. Indeed, it is very likely that you would never be tried or even charged.'

'I am extremely grateful to your Lordship for your opinion. It is not often that a murderer can obtain such authoritative advice before committing a crime. Now, if you will excuse me for a moment, I will make the necessary arrangements.'

He left the judge and went inside the cottage. While he was away, the judge made a quick appreciation of the situation.

Either the man intended to carry out his threat or he did not, but it might be quite impossible to know exactly what his intentions were until too late. The judge made his plan accordingly and, as soon as the man returned from the cottage and placed the shotgun in the judge's hands, with a sudden movement, using all his strength, he turned it on him and shot him dead. The man had thought that he could indulge in a few further taunts at the judge before carrying out his main object and that the judge would be unable to use the shotgun as long as he kept a hand upon the barrel.

Moreover, not only was he unaware of the early weight-putting activities of the judge, but it never occurred to him that, without a word, he would shoot him so unceremoniously.

The judge got up, a little painfully because of his gout, and, having satisfied himself that the stranger would trouble him no more, dragged him, still more painfully, to a place where he was out of view behind some bushes. He put the shotgun beside him and returned to his chair. There was nothing else he could do until his housekeeper returned.

Having sat down, he turned his attention to the sandwiches which Mary had prepared and, between them and the coffee, made a very satisfactory lunch. He then read another article in the *Law Quarterly*, this time upon a question relating to bills of exchange. Later, he had a nap.

Some hours afterwards, Mary returned.

'Did you have a good time?' he asked her.

'Oh yes, indeed, sir,' said Mary. 'It was a lovely time I had. I'll tell you all about it when I've got the supper. But what about you, sir, have you had a good day? Were the sandwiches all right?'

'They were delightful, Mary,' said the judge. 'I ate them all. I never can resist chicken liver. The weather has been gorgeous and your coffee was as good as ever.'

'Well, I am glad, sir,' said Mary. 'Now I'll go and get the supper.' And she started to go into the cottage.

'Oh, before you go,' said the judge, 'there is something I ought to tell you …'

Table Talk

It wasn't the way she said it but what she said. What Eileen said, I mean, not Gladys. I hardly ever listened to what Gladys said. She said so much and she said it all the time, except, of course, when the curtain was up. Oh, her manners were all right. A pretty girl, too. Very pretty. But did she talk? I'm pretty bad myself, but Gladys! Nothing would stop her. On and on she went. She was quite content with an occasional 'Really?' or 'Yes, quite' or the like from me, but it's an awful business putting them in the right places.

Well, it was very difficult for me. I like going out with an attractive girl and you couldn't fault Gladys on looks. She liked me too and was a kind girl. But the strain for most of the evening! I found it quite intolerable.

Then, one day, I hit on the happy idea of taking her to a show. Before that it had been dining out at length or a dance. A show was a brilliant idea. Quick snack before the theatre. Not much chance for her to talk. There wasn't time. Anyway, I was enjoying myself eating and drinking and didn't mind. Then the theatre. We only got there just before the curtain went up and I could manage the two intervals quite easily, particularly as probably one or other of us went out during one of them. After the theatre, supper. More eating and drinking, and the rest of the evening took care of itself. The talk went on whenever it had the chance but it was bearable.

Still I must own I do prefer to talk rather than listen. I don't suppose I'm worse than most men, but I find myself very interesting to talk about to other people. The things I've done, the books I've read and the pictures I've seen, the music I've heard, the views I hold – I like to tell other people about them. I should have liked to have told Gladys. But I never really got the chance. If I began 'There was a book I read the other day …' in she would come with 'Books? Don't talk to me of books. D'you know, the other day I was going through Harridges (or was it Barkleys?) when someone dropped a whole parcel of books on my foot. And d'you know, she never even apologised. You'll never believe what she did say. If I hadn't been so bruised, I'd have laughed. D'you know what …' But by that time I'd given up all hope of telling her about the book I'd read and I'd given up listening. I was just getting ready a 'Good Lord, no really!' or 'Well, well, well,' or 'Everything happens to you, doesn't it?' or something of the kind.

Well, after this sort of thing had been going on for some time, I was beginning to wonder if I could carry on much longer, even though I enjoyed the theatre. We'd seen nearly all the plays worth seeing. Then, suddenly, I met Eileen. At a cocktail party. She was quite different. About talking, I mean. In looks she was quite up to Gladys. But she was a born listener. I talked to her for most of the cocktail party and took her out to dinner. We had a very good evening and I asked her to come out again. She came.

I had now decided to write off Gladys, or, at any rate, put her to reserve. Eileen was the one for me. Lovely figure, face pretty as a picture, and she hardly said a word. I don't mean she was dumb. Oh no. Obviously intelligent. But she just punctuated my remarks appropriately.

And then the blow fell. I didn't notice it at first, not when she said it, I mean. But on the way home. It was the second time I'd taken her out. We'd dined at length and I'd told her quite a lot about myself. She was sweet. And what a listener! I left her at her door and we said good night. She thanked me for a lovely evening and I asked her if she'd like to come out again.

'Oh, I'd love to,' she said, 'but wouldn't it be fun to go to a show next time?'

I Killed Gordon McNaghten

Yes, sir, I once knew a man who had been charged with murder and who was sorry that they pretty well abolished the death penalty in 1957. Not because he preferred to die, oh, dear me, no.

He was fond of life and of the good things in it. So was I. It's a good many years ago since we enjoyed some of them together. But we certainly did.

We saw a lot of each other, Jimmy and I. Had the same tastes in business and pleasure. In both, we liked it easy. Not too much work but well paid. Lots of pleasure and not too much to pay for it. They were good days. At any rate I found them so. Jimmy wasn't quite so lucky. As I said, he found himself charged with murder.

In a way it was a simple case, but it wasn't all that simple. It had been suggested in certain quarters that some of our deals weren't quite on the level. It was nonsense, of course. But Jimmy was heard to remark that, if anyone talked to the police, he wouldn't advise any insurance company to insure that man's life.

Well, Gordon McNaghten went to the police about us. And, before they had time to act on his word of mouth, Gordon McNaghten died. Suddenly and violently.

It was a bad moment for Jimmy. Apart from his statement, there were pieces of evidence which linked him with the murder, and they charged him with it.

He was tried at the Old Bailey and, at the close of the case for the prosecution, things didn't look good for him at all. But I gave him a good alibi, and they couldn't break me down.

I can't say that I told the whole truth, or even the truth at all. But it's not on my conscience. Jimmy was my friend. And friends should stick by each other, don't you think? A little matter of perjury shouldn't come between them. So Jimmy was acquitted.

Why am I telling you all this? Aren't I frightened they can charge me with perjury now? No, sir, I'm not. I shall be standing before the Great Judge long before they can start a case against me, let alone bring me to trial. And I'm not sorry. I've had a full life and a very long one. And I've had enough. The engine's running down.

And perhaps you'll be able to corroborate me when I stand my trial up there, and say that I did tell someone before I left this world. Anyway, I've told you and you can do what you like about it.

But why did Jimmy wish the death penalty hadn't been abolished? I'm coming to that. You mustn't rush me. We like to take it slowly at my age.

Well, we didn't see quite so much of each other, Jimmy and I, after the trial. Both of us thought it might be better for a time at any rate, if we carried on separately. So we drifted apart.

I hadn't heard of him for some years when, one day, I got a shock. I picked up my morning paper. And there was an article by him. And what was it called? 'I Killed Gordon McNaghten.'

I wondered what they paid him for it and I couldn't resist getting in touch with him to ask him. He told me. Then I asked him if it was quite safe. 'Of course it is,' he said. 'I've been acquitted and I can't be tried again for the same crime.' And he was right about that. I asked a lawyer I knew, and he said Yes, that was right, he couldn't be charged again with the same crime.

But some of the public didn't like it and some of the Members of Parliament didn't like it. And a lot of letters were written to the papers and a lot of questions asked in Parliament. And the next I heard of Jimmy was in the paper again. They'd arrested him. Oh, no, the lawyer was quite right. They couldn't charge him with the murder. They didn't. They charged him with two alternative charges: perjury and obtaining money by false pretences.

Jimmy's counsel made a great fuss about the two charges being heard together.

'My Lord,' he said, 'perjury is one thing, false pretences is another. If the prosecution say that my client committed perjury at his trial for murder, let him be tried for that and let the jury give their verdict upon it. If thereafter the prosecution desire to persecute my client by charging him with obtaining money by false pretences, let them do so before a different jury on a different occasion.

'In my respectful submission, my Lord, to try the accused on these two completely separate charges, which are nothing to do with one another, is an affront to justice.'

'Well,' said the judge to counsel for the prosecution, 'what d'you say?'

'My Lord,' replied counsel, 'in the ordinary way the prosecution would not have sought to have had these two different charges heard by the same jury. But this is a very exceptional case. The accused was tried for murder and gave evidence on his own behalf denying his guilt and alleging that he was somewhere else at the time the crime was proved to have been committed. The accused was acquitted.

'Some years later he approached a daily newspaper and offered to sell to it for a not inconsiderable sum a story which he claimed to be true. In this story, secure in the knowledge that he could not be tried again for the murder, he said that he killed Gordon McNaghten and described how he did so. He said his alibi was false and described how he had fabricated it.

'Which story is true, my Lord? The one he swore to in the witness-box, or the one he sold to the newspaper? Suppose, my Lord, the accused is simply tried for perjury, he could go into the witness-box and calmly say that the evidence given by him on his trial for murder was true.

'If the jury accept that explanation and he is then tried for obtaining money from the newspaper proprietors by falsely pretending that he had committed the murder, he could then say that he had committed it. If the jury believed that or were in doubt as to whether it might be true, they would have to acquit him.

'It is true that he could then be charged with perjury on his trial for perjury. But he could then revert to his other story and say that it was the other story which was true.'

Counsel for the prosecution paused. The judge looked thoughtful.

'In other words, as long as the accused is only tried for one of these offences at a time, he can ring the changes until eventually everyone concerned with the case dies of old age. The only solution to this problem, my Lord, is for him to be tried by one and the same jury on both charges as alternatives and that jury can make up its mind on the whole of the evidence as to what the truth of the matter is.

'My learned friend talks of an affront to justice. In my submission, the affront comes from the accused and not from the prosecution. Having sworn he did not commit the murder, he snaps his fingers in the face of the public and arrogantly proclaims that he did commit it. In my submission justice is not so blind that she can't see how to deal with that situation and this is the proper way to deal with it.'

After a little further argument the judge upheld the submission of the prosecution, and Jimmy was tried on three counts for perjury, with an alternative of one count for false pretences.

Apparently the jury believed that he was more truthful in print than he was in the witness-box and, in spite of my evidence (for I supported his alibi again, but less successfully this time), he was convicted of perjury. The judge gave him a sentence of five years on each count – to run consecutively – a total of fifteen years.

In imposing this sentence, the judge said: 'I hope this will be a lesson to you and anyone else who may be minded to laugh at the verdict of a jury in his favour.'

I saw Jimmy before he was taken away. He was wild, I can tell you.

'You must do something about it,' he said to me. 'It's terrible. I shouldn't so much have objected to eighteen months for getting money from the newspaper, but fifteen years for telling the truth! I'd have done better if they'd convicted me of murder the first time. If they hadn't abolished the death penalty, it wouldn't be so bad. But, as it is, I'm worse off than if I'd pleaded guilty to murder. And I'm innocent, Jimmy. You know I am.'

That was the odd thing about the case, sir. Jimmy *was* innocent, completely innocent of murder and perjury. How do I know? Quite simply, because I killed Gordon McNaghten.

No Expectations

Sister Angle, who, at reasonable intervals, had successfully murdered her last eight patients, walked into the offices of Messrs Mendip and Merton, the best-known firm of solicitors in the town where she and her ninth patient were staying. After a short wait, she was shown in to Mr Merton. She explained her business. Her patient, Mrs Gloster, an elderly widow, was in a very frail state of health and wanted to make a will. There was not much time to be lost. Although Mrs Gloster might live for months, or perhaps even a year or two, she was just as likely to die at any moment. Would Mr Merton be good enough to prepare the necessary document at once and bring it to the old lady to execute?

'There isn't much time to be lost,' said Sister Angle, 'though she doesn't know it. Heart, you see.'

'If she doesn't know it,' replied Mr Merton, 'may I ask why she is so anxious to make this will?'

'Because she is – that's all. Old people like making wills. It's quite fun for them sometimes. Cutting out someone they don't like. Putting in someone who'll get a pleasant surprise. They haven't so much to think about, you see. And, however long they're going to live, they're always visualising their death and what people will say about them. But you must know all this. You make the wills and you know the sort of things they do say.'

'Very well,' said Mr Merton, 'I'll take her instructions.'

'I have them here,' said Sister Angle, 'but all the same I think it would be much better if you saw her yourself. She's in full possession of her faculties, but you know the sort of thing that happens when old people die. I should hate to be involved in any trouble. She might leave me a small legacy, for instance, and then her relations might allege that I'd persuaded her to do so. People are so unkind – and greedy. After all I've done for the old lady – night and day I've been with her – it would be little enough if she remembered me in her will – not that I expect anything, mind you, but, if she should happen to be a bit more grateful than most people, I should hate a fuss. So I thought it best to come to a solicitor. If you see her and explain everything, and are satisfied yourself, nothing can go wrong, can it?'

Mr Merton was silent for a moment. London lawyers are apt to have fun at the expense of country solicitors. 'It's a country firm,' says one to another. 'I might have known it,' comes the reply. 'That explains everything.'

But Mr Merton was no fool. He did not at all like the look of Sister Angle. Still less did he like what she had said. Least of all did he like the way she said it. Indeed, he had to remind himself that he shouldn't jump too quickly to conclusions. All the same, he wasn't going to allow an old woman's relatives and friends to be robbed of what was justly theirs.

'Did Mrs Gloster ask you to come to me?' he asked eventually.

'Yes, she did,' said Sister Angle, 'but it was my suggestion. As a matter of fact she didn't like the idea at first. "What do I want with lawyers?" she said. You know the way some people are. But I persuaded her in the end – and,' she paused for the moment and opened her bag. Then: 'She

19

asked me to give you a cheque on account. I believe that's usual when you don't know the client?'

She handed a cheque to Mr Merton. It was for fifteen guineas.

'I made it out,' said Sister Angle, 'but she signed it, of course.'

The signature was shaky but quite legible. Mr Merton took the cheque and paused again. He had read of many similar cases, but had never had one himself. He decided to act for Mrs Gloster – if necessary for nothing. He would not pay the cheque into his bank until he had met her.

'When would Mrs Gloster like to see me?'

'Oh – as soon as you can manage it. Today, if it were possible.'

'Yes, I think that can be done. How about five o'clock? I expect your patient rests after lunch.'

'That would do excellently. We're staying at the Crown.'

'Very well, then – I shall be there.'

Sister Angle got up to go, and then suddenly said: 'How silly of me. I nearly forgot. Here are the instructions for the will.'

She handed a sealed envelope to Mr Merton.

'Did she write them out herself?'

'Oh – yes. She finds it an effort, but, if she takes her time, she can even write a short letter.'

'I see.'

Mr Merton opened the envelope. He felt sure he knew what he was going to see. Everything left to Sister Angle. Indeed, he had even wondered whether he could reconcile it with his conscience to let her be one of the witnesses, for, in that case, she could not legally receive anything which had been left to her. She was not his client and he owed no duty to her. So she could not proceed against him for negligence. All the same, it would be a pretty bad thing for a solicitor to do. Much better to persuade the old lady, if necessary, to change her will.

'D'you know the contents of this envelope?' he asked, as he opened it.

'Certainly not,' said Sister Angle with some asperity. 'What a question to ask!'

'I really don't see why you should take offence. After all, you're looking after Mrs Gloster. She might well have confided in you.'

'Well – she didn't,' said Sister Angle, 'and that's all there is to it.'

Mr Merton unfolded the piece of paper which he had taken from the envelope, and read it.

'I don't want to know what's in it,' said Sister Angle. 'If there's a surprise for me, well I like surprises. And if there isn't, I don't expect anything and I shan't be disappointed. And it's nice not to know.'

'I see your point of view,' said Mr Merton. But he opened the door for the nurse with a greater show of politeness than he had intended before he read his client's instructions. They were simple. 'I wish to leave everything I possess to my niece Norah Carstairs of 52 Norton Hill, London, SW.'

Mr Merton was puzzled. But, perhaps, he thought, the niece is in league with the nurse. Well – he could find that out when he saw Mrs Gloster. So, punctually at five o'clock, he arrived at the *Crown* and was taken by Sister Angle to see her patient.

'I expect you'd like to see Mrs Gloster alone,' said the nurse, when she had introduced them, and she left the room.

'What a sweet woman,' said Mrs Gloster. 'You don't know what I owe her.'

'She seems charming,' said Mr. Merton. He did not mean it, but he was certainly surprised at the genuine affection in Mrs Gloster's voice.

'Night and day she looks after me,' the old lady went on. 'Nothing's too much trouble and never a grumble. I need two nurses really, but she won't hear of it.'

'How nice to find someone like that.'

'Isn't it? And I'm so lucky. I've only had her four or five months. But she treats me as though I were her mother.'

'I'm so glad,' said Mr Merton, and began to think that he really must have misjudged Sister Angle. But there was still the matter of the niece.

'Yes, I was lucky,' went on the old lady. 'I was staying in an hotel where she had a patient and got chatting to her, you know. She told me I ought to have a trained nurse, and I liked her so much I took her address. She wrote to me a week or two later and said that her patient had died, and she's been with me ever since. I have much to be thankful for.'

'Your niece,' asked Mr Merton – 'd'you see much of her?'

'Oh – every so often, you know. Not for some months now, as a matter of fact.'

'Has she ever met Sister Angle?'

'No, as a matter of fact, she hasn't been to see me since Hilda came.'

'Hilda?'

'Sister Angle. But I had a letter from her today. She's coming for a weekend at the end of the month.'

No, thought Mr Merton, there's nothing in this at all. I'm just too suspicious. But it won't be a lesson to me. Too old for that. And then he had another surprise.

'You know,' said Mrs Gloster, 'I'd have dearly liked to leave something to Hilda, but she wouldn't hear of it. I

22

just mentioned the subject casually to her and she was quite upset. And I'm sure it would really hurt her feelings if I did. She'd feel that I'd thought that all the love and affection she'd shown me was with an ulterior motive.'

Mr Merton found this a little difficult to reconcile with some of the things Sister Angle had said to him. But all he thought was: serve the woman right; if she's laid on the butter too thick and the old lady's taken her at her word, so much the worse for her. I didn't like her anyway.

'So,' went on Mrs Gloster, 'I've simply had to leave her out. It'd be like tipping the manager of a hotel in mistake for the head waiter if I did anything else. And I couldn't bear to hurt her. Don't you think I'm right?'

'Absolutely,' said Mr Merton, with conviction. 'I've drawn the will for you and, if you like, I'll get Sister Angle to come and witness it with me. If she knows anything about the law, she'll know that must mean you've left her nothing.'

'How kind you are,' said Mrs Gloster.

Mr Merton fetched Sister Angle and together they watched Mrs Gloster sign the will. Then they both signed the attestation clause.

'There, that's done,' said Sister Angle cheerfully, 'and now we needn't talk about such morbid things any more. Mrs Gloster will live to be a hundred!'

But she was dead in a week.

When Mr Merton heard of Mrs Gloster's death, he made it his business to get into communication with her niece. He felt uncomfortable about the case. But an interview with the niece convinced him that she had no connection whatever with Sister Angle and that the nurse had received no benefit whatever, direct or indirect, from the death of her patient. Indeed, she had lost by it. She was out of a job. All the same, when Mr Merton met the doctor who had attended Mrs Gloster he asked him about her.

'Oh – are you interested in the lady?' asked the doctor.

'Oh – no – not really, but I made her will a few days before she died.'

'You lawyers!' said the doctor. 'Oh – no, you didn't say it, but I know what you're after. Well – you can set your mind at rest – there'll be no post-mortems or inquests on Mrs Gloster. I don't care who she left her money to. Just an ordinary heart case. Here today, gone tomorrow. It's as good a way as any, if you ask me. You're not going to tell me she left me a small legacy, I suppose?'

'I'm afraid not. She left everything to her niece.'

'Well – what are you worrying about?'

'Oh – nothing really – but I didn't much like the nurse – a queer fish.'

'I thought she was a darned good nurse. Her patient adored her. Wonder she didn't leave her something.'

Mr Merton was on the point of mentioning the strange reason why nothing was left to Sister Angle when he realised that it would be a breach of professional confidence. So he contented himself with saying: 'Yes – I agree about that. Oh, well – it just shows how dangerous it is to rely on hunches.'

But he remained puzzled.

Meanwhile, Sister Angle had fixed herself up with another job. This time it was as nurse to an old gentleman. She had found him in one of the more expensive hotels where the majority of guests walk with sticks, have deaf aids or are wheeled about in bath chairs. Their voices are quavery and their subjects of conversation almost non-existent. They have nothing really to live for but do not want to die. From time to time they eat too much and are sick.

'I shouldn't have had that lobster. It never agrees with me. But there are so few pleasures I get.'

They are very pathetic, these old people, and it was really a kindness on the part of Sister Angle to help them on their way out. But she did not do it with that in mind. Her object was simple and ordinary – to make enough money during her working life to enable her to live in comfort when she no longer felt like working. Her plan of campaign was by no means complicated, but it was far from ordinary. First, she selected her victim. There was not much difficulty in this. There is a shortage of trained nurses and most old people respond quickly to kind treatment. She only took on heart cases. They could have other things as well, but the heart had to be liable to stop suddenly. Her patients did not have to be wealthy, provided they were very comfortably off. She treated her victims with the utmost care and kindness, so that they were really as happy as possible during the short remainder of their lives.

Now, Sister Angle, although not particularly intelligent, was well aware that greed is the ruin of most criminals. The blackmailer goes to his victim once too often, the burglar goes to houses in the same street, the perpetrator of a long-term fraud cheats his victim of too much. She was also well aware that, if a wealthy patient dies and leaves everything, or even a substantial legacy, to the nurse, relatives tend to be displeased and even to make enquiries. Her motto was 'little and often'.

What she did was simply this. She ingratiated herself to such an extent with her patient that she obtained, during the patient's lifetime, in addition to her salary – at the full standard rate for trained nurses – either by plain theft or a succession of gifts, or a mixture of the two, some reasonable sum – such as £200 to £300. The minimum was £100. The maximum £500. The period over which she collected it never exceeded six months. On the rare occasions when, by an error of judgment, she selected a victim who kept too tight a hold on the purse strings, she made some excuse for leaving, and left. But she was careful to part on good terms and after giving a full week's notice.

But she did not often have to leave and her last nine patients, including Mrs Gloster, had stayed the full course. Her methods of obtaining small sums of money from her patients were many and varied. For example, if her patients were well enough, she would suggest that they went to a race-meeting. She would then persuade them to bet on horses which she normally named after the race was over. The stake, of course, went into her pocket. She was, however, quite as good at getting money out of her patients by persuading them to give it to her as by stealing it, and it was never a large sum at a time, unless there was an excellent excuse for it. She made certain that, when her dead victim's pass-book was examined, there would be no items which, if enquiry were made, could not be satisfactorily explained.

In fact, enquiries had never been made. The total amount spent was so small compared with the estate that no one had ever bothered about it, and she made quite sure that none of the estate was left to her. In the result, all she received, after her patient had died, were the grateful thanks of the beneficiaries, and occasionally a present. She considered it necessary to kill her patients because, in her view, there was no safe alternative. If she simply stayed with them till they died natural deaths, the amount she would have received might be so large a sum as to cause enquiry. If she left a patient after, say, six months, her successor might bring to light her defalcations or the patient, even, might discover them.

Her method of killing her patients was as kind as her treatment of them. She had saved up, over the years, large quantities of sleeping drugs. She obtained these by the simple expedient of asking doctors for prescriptions for her patients and either not giving them the tablets or telling the doctor, for example, that the patient had been having two a night when, in fact, only one had been given. In consequence, she had many lethal doses in her possession and, when she considered the time was ripe, she tucked her patient up in bed, administered the necessary dose, and sent for the doctor in the morning.

There was usually no difficulty in persuading her patients to swallow the required number of tablets, but sometimes she dissolved them. It was really too simple. In the morning the doctor came and found his patient dead. He had been ready for this to happen for months and the thought of refusing a certificate never occurred to him. They were plain cases. The only risk Sister Angle ran was the possibility of such a refusal and the consequent post-mortem, and this risk she reduced to a minimum by her method of obtaining her patient's money and her care never to take too much and to make sure that the patient made a will just before he or she died under which nothing whatever was left to her.

It became a matter of routine. But, even so, she was careful never to overreach herself, and occasionally refused to let her patient give her too substantial a present at one time. She had no conscience to trouble her, and, even if she had, the devil could, no doubt, have come to her aid by pointing out the happiness enjoyed by her victims in their last months and their peaceful manner of dying – always in their sleep.

Mr Bruton-Trent was her last victim, a charming old man of eighty-five, whose heart still kept beating, though it was difficult to think why. He was an admirable subject for Sister Angle, and she even took a considerable liking to the old gentleman. It was reciprocated to such an extent that she did for one short moment think of allowing him to marry her. But, even before she learned that he still had a wife alive, some fifteen years younger than himself, she had dismissed the notion as too dangerous. If you can reach eighty-five with a heart firing on only one out of four cylinders, you may just as likely reach a hundred and if after marrying him, she stopped the one cylinder firing, there was always the danger that a relative might object. When eventually he told her about his wife, she was glad she had already made the decision not to marry him. She hated disappointments.

'Yes,' he said, when he first mentioned Louisa Bruton-Trent's existence, 'I feel rather bad about not telling you before.'

'Why should you? It's none of my business.'

'Ah!' said the old man. 'I know that now, but I didn't when I first met you. I owe you an apology, my dear. I wish I'd met you before Louisa, I must say. We might have been very happy. You don't mind an old man burbling away like this, do you?'

'Of course not. You just say anything that comes into your head. It's good for you.'

After four-and-a-half months with Mr Bruton-Trent, Sister Angle decided that she – and her patient – must be moving on. She had quite easily obtained some £400 off the old man, and she felt that, if she went on much longer, she might be tempted to exceed the limit. So she duly sought out the best-known local solicitor in the district where they were living. This was nowhere near the town where Mr Merton of Mendip and Merton practised. She was careful about this, too. First she prepared for the execution of the will. Her patients usually wanted to make some provision for her and, naturally, Mr Bruton-Trent was no exception. But she persuaded him in the end, obtained his instructions to leave half his estate to his widow and the other half to a grand-nephew, and presented these instructions to Mr Bland of Bland and Bland.

Mr Bland was not a suspicious person like Mr Merton, and he had no intuitive feelings about Sister Angle. On the contrary, when he and his clerk went to Mr Bruton-Trent's bedside for the execution of the will, he was able to agree quite truthfully that she seemed a charming woman. He thought no less of her a week later when he was informed of her patient's death. He was accordingly horrified when, about a month afterwards, an inspector of police called on him and asked him for a statement as to the circumstances in which the deceased had made his last will. He was even more horrified when he was informed that Sister Angle was being charged with his murder. He had only met the nurse twice, but not only had he thought her a nice woman, an admirable nurse and one to whom her patient was obviously devoted, but he himself had special knowledge which, in his view, would undoubtedly clear Sister Angle of any suspicion. He proceeded to explain this to the inspector.

'Inspector,' he said, 'this must surely be a horrible mistake.'

'I don't think so, sir,' said the inspector.

'Well – see if this alters your opinion. It's Mrs Bruton-Trent, the widow, I imagine, who is responsible for all this?'

'She certainly started the ball rolling, sir,' said the inspector, 'but she was executrix of her late husband's will and, in the circumstances, it isn't surprising she came to us – and just as well, if I may say so.'

The inspector at that time knew that a lethal dose of seconal had been found inside Mr Bruton-Trent and that the only person who could have given it to him was Sister Angle. But Mr Bland was not yet aware of this and he went on: 'I don't know what evidence you have, but just you listen to this – or there may be a grave miscarriage of justice. The instructions Sister Angle brought me for the will were that the estate was to be divided in half – half to the widow and half to a grand-nephew.'

'I know,' said the inspector. 'Sister Angle has told us. If you could have seen her face, when we told her that that had been changed, you might have thought a bit differently.'

Mr Bruton-Trent's last will, with the omission of formal and immaterial parts, read as follows: 'I appoint my wife Louisa, whom I have not seen or wanted to see for years, as executrix of this my will. That is the only thing she will have ever done for me. I give everything I possess to that dear, sweet woman Hilda Angle, who has made my life so incomparably happy. It will be my wife's duty, as executrix, to collect in the estate and give it to Hilda. I wish I could see her doing it.'

When Mr Bland and his clerk had called on the testator he had made them promise not to tell Sister Angle that the will they had prepared was to be scrapped and that, instead, one in her favour which he had written out himself was to be executed. 'Executed', incidentally, is the right word with which to end the story of Sister Angle.

I'm Afraid

Ernest Turnweather didn't like it. He didn't like the idea at all. But at first he concealed his fears and tried to master them himself.

'There's nothing in it,' he told himself as he was shaving. 'It's absurd to be worried about it,' he added as he had his bath. 'It happens to hundreds of people,' he said aloud as he dressed.

His wife was passing the open bedroom door at the time and was interested to know what he was thinking about. So she went in.

'What happens to hundreds of people?' she asked. And that was the end of Ernest trying to be strong-minded. He had been longing to admit his fears to his wife from the beginning but felt he owed it to his pride at least to try to overcome them. But, when she asked point-blank, the temptation was too great.

'Oh, it's nothing,' he said, as though the question had been, 'What's the matter?' But, lest she should accept his answer and go away, he added quickly: 'It's only that I'm a bit worried about this manipulation. It's stupid, I know.'

'But, darling, there's really nothing in it.'

'I know,' he said. 'I know there isn't. I've told myself so a hundred times.'

'A hundred times! You poor darling, you have been worrying.'

Elsie was a sympathetic wife and he felt much happier now that she knew his fears. He went on to elaborate.

'It says in a book I saw in the library,' he said, 'that it's quite easy to break a neck if the fellow goes the wrong way about it.'

'But, darling, your man has been trained to go the right way about it.'

'I know,' said Ernest, 'but this book says that a qualified surgeon once tore the ... the ... wait a moment, I wrote it down.'

He searched for his notebook, found it and opened up the reference.

'Here it is,' he went on. 'He tore the dentate ligament and caused the odontoid process to be forced posteriorly into the spinal cord at the level of the axis vertebra.'

'And what did he get for that?' said Elsie, trying to lighten the tone of the conversation.

'I don't know what he got, but the patient died.'

'And the surgeon was qualified?'

'Certainly.'

'Well, accidents must happen, of course, but ...'

'Exactly,' said Ernest. 'Accidents must happen. Why not to me?'

'But they're terribly unlikely, I'm sure. One in a million. You never worried when you had that trouble with your knee. If there'd been an accident then, you might have had a stiff knee for life. D'you remember, the surgeon even warned us that it was a delicate operation and there was just a chance the knee might be left stiff. I thought at the time that was to cover him in case he made a mess of it.'

'So did I, but that was quite different. If I *had* had a stiff knee I could still enjoy life. We could still go to theatres and concerts. We should still have each other. Just a slightly more limited life, that's all. But just as long. But if they make a mistake with the neck – well, I mean to say – that's why they hang people, isn't it, because the neck's a nice convenient thing to break, and, if you break it, a hundred to one you kill the man. I have heard of people living with a broken neck, but there can't be many of them.'

'Now there's going to be no mistake. Hundreds of people are manipulated as you're going to be.'

'That's what I was telling myself when you came in.'

'Oh yes, of course.'

'It happens to hundreds of people, I said.'

'Well, so it does. And they all come out alive.'

'No, not all. What about the man who had his … his …' – he picked up his notebook – 'his dentate ligament torn and his odontoid process forced posteriorly into the spinal cord. Posteriorly! It sounds horrible.'

'You shouldn't have gone to the library, darling. You know quite well that anyone who reads a medical book thinks he has all the diseases under the sun.'

'You're quite right, darling. I feel a blithering idiot. But each time I tell myself that, some other part of me says: "But you want to live, don't you? You're not ready to be put to sleep yet!"'

'You really mustn't be so morbid, darling. Let's go out to dinner tonight somewhere, and forget all about the beastly manipulation. This time next week it'll be all over.'

'No, it won't. It's eight days exactly. I've got to wait till 11.30 tomorrow week. Think of it. And then they're usually late. Keep you waiting in a beastly room with out-of-date magazines I don't want to read.'

'At least they aren't medical books. Of course they couldn't leave those about or it would double the symptoms of every patient. But look, darling, I tell you what. Before we go out tonight, we'll pop in and see Gerald for ten minutes. I'm sure he'll say something soothing. And after all he does know what he's talking about.'

Gerald was a friend of theirs, a general practitioner with very high qualifications.

Ernest felt a little better after telling his wife, but horrible thoughts kept returning to him whenever he wasn't compelled to concentrate on something.

He tried to read the paper in the train on the way to the office, but, before long, the train's movement started to jerk out: 'Thursday-week – Thursday-week – Thursday-week – Thursday-week,' and as the speed increased, 'broken-his-neck, broken-his-neck, broken-his-neck,' so that he was quite glad when a carriage bore asked him if he'd heard this one.

Once in the office he was compelled to take his mind off his own affairs for most of the time, but even there something had to happen to make him return to them.

'You're not looking so good, Mr Turnweather,' said his secretary, a cheerful girl with a very slight cockney accent. 'Are you feeling all right?'

'Oh – yes – quite, thanks. At least – I've got to have a beastly manipulation next week. It's got me down a bit, I suppose.'

'Manipulation? My sister's a physiotherapist. Might I ask where? I'm sure she'd be interested.'

He fingered his tie.

'The neck,' he said, 'as a matter of fact.'

'Let's hope they don't break it,' said his secretary.

'That would be a pity,' he managed to say with a forced smile.

'Shouldn't see you here much after that, I shouldn't imagine. We'd miss you, though.'

'Thank you. That's kind of you. Now might I have those invoices?'

The next day his secretary informed him that she'd talked over his case with her sister.

'Something funny she told me,' she said. 'I'd never believe you could live with a broken neck, but you can, she said.'

'Indeed?'

'Oh yes. When she was in hospital they brought in a man with a broken neck. In her ward too. He lived for three days.'

'Really?'

'Three whole days. Can't have been very comfortable. I'd prefer to be killed straight off, wouldn't you, Mr Turnweather?'

'I'd prefer not to be killed at all, Miss Banks.'

'But if you had to be ... I mean ...'

'I think I'd like to speak to Mr Dixon,' Ernest said firmly.

His wife had not been able to fix up a meeting with Gerald for three days, but then they went and had coffee with him.

Elsie started the subject.

'Ernest wants to know if it's really worth having this manipulation,' she said. 'He hardly feels any pain now at all.'

'Then he's worrying about it,' said Gerald.

'I remember when I was a boy, I was on the operating table waiting to have my appendix out. Just before I had the anaesthetic the pain disappeared, completely disappeared. Wonderful thing nature. I was frightened of the operation – so the pain disappeared. No pain, no operation. Fortunately they took no notice, operated, and just managed to save my life.'

'I don't mind pain,' said Ernest. 'Not in reason, that is. I could get along with this if it were necessary.'

'But it isn't necessary, my dear boy. You've just got a misplaced cervical disc and it's brushing up against a nerve. Put the disc back in its proper place and bang goes the pain. It's as simple as that.'

'Ernest was worrying in case the man made a mistake and broke his neck.'

'Well, that can happen, of course,' said Gerald quite cheerfully, 'but you've a good two-to-one chance.'

Then, seeing that his humour was as misplaced as Ernest's disc, he hurriedly added: 'I was only joking, old boy. Silly of me. I'm sorry. I personally have never known a case of a manipulation of this kind by a qualified practitioner being fatal. Not one. Does that make you feel better?'

'How many cases have you known about in all?'

'Altogether? Let me see,' said Gerald, wondering how big a lie he could tell without it being obvious. 'If you include the time I was a student I'd say – many thousand. Many thousand,' he added with emphasis. He was trying hard to make up for his original bad taste.

'So that there isn't really any chance of a – of a mishap?' said Ernest. 'No real chance at all?'

'None.'

'But what about this chap I read about who ...' – and Ernest got out his notebook – 'whose dentate ligament was torn, with the result that the odontoid process was forced into the spinal cord. Posteriorly,' he added.

'Don't use such long words, old boy. Poppycock.'

'But there was such a case. The book said so.'

'Well, of course – a surgeon is only human ... and every now and then, I suppose ...'

'Then you admit that it is possible he might – might break my neck?' said Ernest, determined to add to his own

36

fears. Fear is like that. Like cigarettes or opium. You must have more of it.

'Much less likely than that, on the way back from your *successful* manipulation, a motor car will mow you down.'

'I'd thought of that too,' said Ernest, 'but pretty well every time I drive I see some kind of an accident. I shouldn't like to think that my chances were no better than that.'

Eventually Gerald and Elsie persuaded him to talk about something else but, when he went to bed, Ernest took two sleeping tablets or he would have had little sleep.

The next morning at the office he was greeted brightly by his secretary.

'I've got some good news for you, Mr Turnweather,' she said. 'My sister says they've just invented a drug which makes manipulation quite unnecessary. You just inject it and somehow or other it pushes the disc back into place. She says the manipulators will be out of work once this thing is on the market.'

'I take it,' said Ernest with some irony, 'that it is not likely to be on the market before next Thursday?'

'Have a heart, Mr Turnweather,' said his secretary; 'it's only just invented. And in America. My sister thinks it'll be two or three years before it gets over here. That's if it stands up to the tests.'

'Then why, may I ask,' said Ernest, 'why is it good news for me? My neck is to be broken next Thursday. Not in three years' time.'

'I thought you'd be pleased for people who won't have to be manipulated in three years. You were so worried yourself I thought you'd be pleased for the other people.'

'I'm very pleased for the other people,' he said. 'Very pleased indeed.' Then a thought occurred to him.

'Would you mind going out and getting me some cigarettes? I've come without any.'

As soon as she was gone, he telephoned his wife. 'Look, darling,' he said, 'I've just heard of a new drug which makes these manipulations unnecessary. I wonder if you'd see Gerald about it?'

'What's it called?'

'Well, I don't know, but he's bound to. He's very up to date. It isn't actually on the market yet – but I don't see why I shouldn't wait till it is. After all – it would avoid missing a day at the office.'

'Only half a day, darling. They say you'll be quite all right to go to work in the afternoon.'

'Well, half a day, then. My work is quite important, you know. Something urgent might happen while I was being manipulated.'

'When will this drug be available?'

'I don't know exactly, but my secretary – her sister's a physiotherapist, you know – she said about three years.'

'Three years!' said his wife. 'You don't mean it?'

'I don't see why not.'

'Look, darling, Thursday will be here and over before you know where you are. I should change that secretary of yours if she's going to say silly things like that.'

'She was only trying to be helpful.'

'Then she wants her brains tested,' said Elsie. 'Now, you must pull yourself together, darling. It's only a couple more days.'

On the way home the people in his carriage were discussing a particularly bad murder case.

'I'd hang the man *myself*,' said one man.

'I shouldn't mind pulling a lever or pressing a button, but I shouldn't like the preliminaries,' said another.

38

'Putting the thing round his neck or whatever it is. What d'you feel about it?' and the speaker looked at Ernest.

'I don't believe in hanging,' he said firmly. 'Who are we to take away another man's life?'

'He took someone else's.'

'Then you would steal from a thief, would you?' said Ernest rather warmly. The question had annoyed him. 'You would burn down the house of a man who committed arson? An eye for an eye, a tooth for a tooth.'

'And a neck for a neck,' added a third. 'I don't see why not. I'd hang the fellow, tie him up, put the thing on his head, frogmarch him to the platform and pull the lever. The whole works.'

'You're not an executioner by any chance?' asked Ernest offensively.

'Well, in a way, you might say I am,' replied the man. 'I'm an orthopaedic surgeon.'

'I say – are you feeling all right?' asked the man opposite Ernest.

Ernest had gone white.

'It's nothing,' he replied, 'I get these turns occasionally. I wonder if you'd mind opening the window a bit more.'

Someone obliged.

'As a matter of fact,' Ernest went on, 'I've an appointment with one of your tribe tomorrow. Just a disc being replaced.'

'Too many discs being replaced,' said the surgeon. 'Don't believe in it myself. Not in half the cases, that is.'

'Then don't you think I ought to have mine done?'

'Well, my dear chap, I don't know much about you, do I, except that apparently you don't believe in capital punishment and are said to have a misplaced disc. Who's the surgeon, may I ask? Surprised he hasn't done it already, if it had to be done.'

Ernest mentioned a name.

'Oh,' said the surgeon, 'I see.' He paused for a moment. 'Actually,' he went on, 'I suppose I shouldn't discuss a colleague's case, should I? Who's going to win the big race at Ascot? Anyone any ideas?'

As soon as he got home Ernest said to his wife: 'We must get hold of Gerald at once. I met a fellow in the train – an orthopaedic surgeon – and he obviously thinks nothing of this chap who's doing me.'

'What was his name?'

'After what he said I didn't like to ask him. Might have looked as though I were going to cook up a libel action or something. But another thing too. He thinks half these manipulations are all wrong. We must check up with Gerald.'

'But, darling, we have checked up with Gerald. He says you couldn't go to a better man. He knows him well.'

'Yes, that's true. He did say that. I wish I knew the name of the chap in the train. I know – I'll ring Tomlinson. He travels with us every day. Just a chance he might know him.'

But Tomlinson did not know him. 'Never seen him before. But seemed a knowledgeable chap, didn't he? I nearly asked him his name, in case anything happened to me. I like these chaps who don't believe in operations and manipulations – even though it's against their interest to say so. I'd trust a fellow like that. He didn't seem to think much of your fellow, did he? Funny. Didn't seem to be the sort of chap who'd indulge in professional jealousy. Sure your man's all right?'

At last 11.30 on Thursday arrived and the surgeon did not keep Ernest waiting. He was a jovial-looking man, abounding in confidence.

'Well, we shan't be very long, I hope,' he said. 'Ever had anything like this before?'

'Not on the neck,' said Ernest.

'Well, there's nothing in it. You'll just hear a click. May be quite a loud one like this.'

He cracked the joints of his fingers in a way that made Ernest wince.

'Or like this,' the surgeon added, and he snapped his fingers loudly.

'I doubt if it'll hurt, but, if it does, it'll only be for a moment.'

'Quite,' said Ernest.

'There's one thing I must warn you of, though. I have to grip you rather firmly. Don't resist, please, or it could be dangerous.'

'Dangerous!' said Ernest.

'I might break your neck.'

'You mean,' said Ernest, 'that you might tear the dentate ligament and cause the odontoid process to be forced into the spinal cord at the level of the axis vertebra.'

'Posteriorly,' added the surgeon almost automatically, and then his face suddenly showed interested and considerable surprise. 'Good gracious,' he said, 'you must have been reading "Polgrave on Fractures".'

'I glanced at it,' said Ernest, apologetically.

'How very odd,' said the surgeon. 'It's the first time I've had a patient who's read the book. But, as you have, I'll tell you something that'll interest you. That case he mentioned, where the fellow's neck was broken, was his own case.'

'Really?' said Ernest.

'The patient knew nothing, of course, but it upset Polgrave a good deal. All the same he was a great man. As a matter of fact I did all my orthopaedic training under

41

him. Every bit. Now perhaps you'd kindly remove your shirt and collar.'

The Lesson

The prisoner had been acquitted and the judge, Mr Justice Streak, thereupon addressed him as follows: 'William Pellet, the jury, who are the sole judges of the facts have acquitted you and accordingly you are discharged. But I feel bound to add that in my opinion you have been very lucky in your jury. I hope at any rate that you will have learned your lesson from these proceedings.'

William Pellet left the dock and, after having celebrated his acquittal in a normal manner, he went to a firm of solicitors.

'What right has he to talk to me like that?' he asked the partner who interviewed him. 'The jury acquitted me, and he sends me away with a stain on my character. Look at this evening paper. "Acquitted prisoner lucky in his jury." That looks nice at home, doesn't it? Will I get my job back? I don't know.'

'I sympathise very much,' said the solicitor, 'but what advice are you asking me for?'

'Why can't I sue him for slander?'

'You can't sue a judge – or counsel, for that matter – for anything they say in Court.'

'What – not even for a private remark? If a barrister turned round and spoke to his client and someone overheard him slander someone, couldn't he be sued?'

'Ah, but that wouldn't be in the course of the proceedings.'

'Nor was this. The jury had said Not Guilty. The judge had discharged me. What right had he to go and smear my name, just to get his own back because the jury weren't his way of thinking?'

'Well,' said the solicitor, 'I can only say that some judges – not many – do it from time to time. Personally I don't think they should, but I can't see an action for slander succeeding. It would be struck out without a trial.'

'Are you sure?'

'I'm never sure about anything without counsel's opinion, and not always with, but that's what I think.'

'Would you be prepared to have a go and see what happened?'

The solicitor thought for a moment. Eventually he said: 'I must consult my partners about this, but, if they agree, I've no objection to writing a letter making a claim and then issuing a writ. But I warn you you'll lose and have to pay not only our costs but the judge's as well.'

'Will it get into the papers?'

'If it gets to the Court of Appeal, it will, but that'll be expensive.'

'I don't care,' said Mr Pellet. 'It's so damned unfair. I feel sore about it. I'd give a good deal to get even with that judge. You can spend up to £100. Here's fifty of them now.' Mr Pellet started to count out fifty one-pound notes, but the solicitor stopped him.

'We shan't need anything like that to begin with. Of course, if we take it to the Court of Appeal it would probably cost the best part of it. But £10 on account will do very well for the moment.'

'You have the fifty while I've got it,' said Mr Pellet. 'I want the judge to know I mean business. And, if you know it, it's more likely that he will.'

In consequence of this interview, Mr Justice Streak eventually received the following letter from Messrs Pale and Woolley.

The Hon. Mr Justice Streak,
Royal Courts of Justice,
Strand, WC2.

Personal and Confidential

Dear Sir,

We write with regret and some embarrassment on behalf of our client Mr William Pellet. Our client, who was recently acquitted after a trial presided over by you at the Central Criminal Court, complains that after you had discharged him you said to him in Court: "You have been very lucky in your jury. I hope at any rate that you will have learned your lesson from these proceedings." Our client complains that by those words you meant and were understood to mean that he was in fact guilty of the offence of which he had been acquitted, and he further instructs us to put forward the contention that, as the trial was over and he had been discharged, the words were not spoken by you in your judicial capacity and were accordingly not privileged. Our client instructs us to ask you whether you are prepared to make a public apology and withdrawal and to pay a reasonable sum by way of damages. In the event of your not being prepared to comply with this request, our instructions are to issue a writ and we shall be glad to know if we are right in our assumption that the Treasury Solicitor will accept service of proceedings on your behalf.

We need only add that we are naturally very sorry to have to write to you in these terms, but, although we fully appreciate that there may be a complete answer to our client's claim, it seemed to us that it was right that the claim should be put forward.

We are,

Your obedient servants,

Pale and Woolley.

Within a week of the letter being received by the judge the Treasury Solicitor wrote back that he would accept service of any proceedings but that an immediate application would be made to strike them out on the ground that any statement of the judge was absolutely privileged. Mr Pellet instructed his solicitors to issue the writ and within a fortnight Master Trotter had, on the application of the Treasury Solicitor, struck out the proceedings. Mr Pellet appealed to the judge in Chambers, who upheld the Master's decision but gave leave to appeal. In consequence, the Court of Appeal in due course gave their decision on the matter. Lord Justice Rowe, who delivered the unanimous judgment of the Court, said, among other things: 'We cannot doubt but that anything said by a judge in open Court relating to the proceedings in purported pursuance of his capacity as a judge must be absolutely privileged. The law places great trust in and imposes great responsibilities on judges, and an absolute privilege is essential to the proper discharge of their judicial functions. At the same time, we all feel that in cases where for example, as here, the defence is an alibi it is highly undesirable that a judge, after a verdict of acquittal, should say anything which reflects adversely on the acquitted person. In cases where the *admitted* conduct of the acquitted prisoner has been negligent, reckless, wrong or ill-advised, it may well be that a few words of advice or comment from the judge may be in the prisoner's or the public interest. But it can never be right in our view for a judge to cast doubt upon the correctness of a verdict of Not Guilty. Having said that, we nevertheless have no alternative but to dismiss this appeal with costs.'

Now the Court of Appeal does not normally have any concern with criminal cases. Criminal appeals come before the Court of Criminal Appeal, and a former Lord Chief Justice once said that that Court can, if it thinks fit, disregard the views of the Court of Appeal in favour of its own. Mr Justice Streak, who was a judge of the CCA, did not at all agree with the criticisms which the Court of Appeal had made upon him, nor did one or two other judges of that Court, including Mr Justice Crane. That judge remarked that, whatever the Court of Appeal might say, he was going to please himself as to what he said in his own Court, an opinion which Mr Justice Streak heartily endorsed.

Mr Pellet, on the other hand, was wholly unsatisfied with the mere words which had fallen from the Court of Appeal. That did not make up to him for what the judge had done. It later transpired that a Court reporter heard him remark, after the appeal was dismissed: 'I'll be even with him yet.'

Mr Justice Streak lived alone in a small house in London. One night, a few months after Mr Pellet's appeal had been dismissed, two men managed to obtain entrance to the judge's house. With masks on their faces they entered his bedroom. He was in bed. They got him out of bed, stripped him and then proceeded to tar and feather him. They then deposited him on the steps of his house, with a printed card above his head: 'Not so lucky this time', and made off.

After a comparatively short time Mr Justice Streak was found by a policeman and conveyed by ambulance to hospital. He had a very unpleasant time indeed, but fully recovered in the end. Within a few hours of his having been discovered, a detective-inspector, accompanied by a sergeant, called on Mr Pellet and invited him to account for his movements that night.

'Since when have I had to account to the police for my movements?' he said. 'Go away, please. I don't like you.'

'Someone has just tarred and feathered Mr Justice Streak. Do you know anything about it?' persisted the inspector.

'Well, that's the best news I've heard for years,' said Mr Pellet. 'How did he take it?'

'We have reason to believe that you were concerned in this very serious assault.'

'Indeed? Then, no doubt, if you have sufficient evidence, you will arrest me. If you haven't, please go away. I want to get back to sleep. Perhaps I should add that, much as I should like the credit for teaching the old man a lesson, it was nothing to do with me.'

'Can you suggest who it might have been?'

'If I could, I wouldn't. But, if he treats everyone as he treated me, I can imagine that there's quite a long list of candidates. Now, if you don't mind, I'd be glad if you'd go. There's a draught and I'm sleepy.'

The police officers went away, and Mr Pellet went back to bed. They then interviewed the judge's temporary housekeeper and they were luckier in the information they obtained from her. As a result of it they began to build up quite a substantial case against Mr Pellet. Eventually it was considered that there was sufficient evidence to justify a charge of assault occasioning actual bodily harm against Mr Pellet, and he was accordingly arrested. As the proceedings went on at the Magistrate's Court, the evidence against Mr Pellet increased and by the time he had been committed for trial to the Old Bailey there was a formidable case against him.

Mr Justice Crane was the judge and his summing-up told heavily against the prisoner. But nevertheless the judge was careful to say in the course of his direction to the jury: 'Although, members of the jury, an assault of this kind upon a man of Mr Justice Streak's years must be a very serious matter – indeed, it might easily have resulted in his death – nevertheless you must not in any way be influenced by the fact that this disgraceful attack was perpetrated upon a distinguished High Court judge. The only question you have to decide is whether the prisoner is one of the men responsible. It matters not whether the person assaulted was a judge or a crossing-sweeper. You will consider simply whether the evidence convinces you that the prisoner is guilty.' The judge went on to review the evidence and, by the time he had finished, there were few people who did not expect a verdict of guilty, in spite of the prisoner's emphatic denials. At last the jury retired to consider their verdict. They returned after three hours with a verdict of Not Guilty. Mr Justice Crane looked severely at them and then said: 'William Pellet, the jury have found you Not Guilty, and you are discharged. In my opinion you are – ' He paused.

'Yes?' said Mr Pellet enquiringly.

'Discharged,' said the judge. 'Call the next case.'

The Adjutant Who Knew Too Much

If you're in the Army in wartime and have had anything to do with the law in civilian life, you are liable to be pressed into service by anyone, from the CO to the sanitary man. I am referring to those who have been on the right side of the law – in a solicitor's office, in the Temple or something of that kind. But, in fact, use can be made of those who have been on the other side of the law. Burglars, for example, can be very helpful in an emergency, and, indeed, acting on a well-known principle, I once recommended that a burglar be made a provost lance-corporal. The strain of having to distinguish between his own and other people's property, however, proved too much for him.

But, if you've been respectably in the law, it is assumed by everyone that no legal problem is too difficult for you. If anyone is to be court-martialled, you will be detailed to defend him, poor fellow. If some knotty legal question arises, your advice will be sought. Protestations that the particular aspect of law concerned is not in your line will help you not a jot. You've been in the law, you know it all.

Well, I had been connected with the law before I went into the Army and, what is more, I thought I knew something about it. I made no modest protests and I willingly placed my knowledge and experience at the disposal of anyone who chose to ask for my help.

One of the first cases I came across in the Orderly Room was a file labelled 'The Elusive Private X'. He had gone absent without leave, had been arrested and brought back to the battalion, had escaped, was again arrested and brought back. Again he escaped and again he was recaptured. I was given the job of prosecuting him for desertion. In order to prove his guilt the prosecution had to show that he intended to remain permanently away from the Army. His persistent escapes strongly suggested that he did not intend to return. Private X, however, gave various reasons why, each time he escaped, he had especially wanted to go home – just for the moment. The fact that, as soon as the police arrived at the place where he was living, he got out through a back window he explained as being due to panic and a prejudice against the police.

I need hardly say that I disposed of these pitiful defences with no difficulty at all, and he was sentenced to a substantial term of imprisonment or detention.

During the period while he was awaiting an escort to take him away my commanding officer had him put in handcuffs.

I was then the assistant adjutant and very respectfully I protested to the CO.

'You can't keep a man in handcuffs, sir,' I said. 'It's illegal.'

'If I don't, he'll escape again,' said the CO.

'Not if he's properly guarded, sir,' I said.

'Well,' said the CO, 'we'll go and see him.'

So we visited Private X, who confirmed my view that he did not like wearing handcuffs. He described them as uncomfortable and limiting his movements.

'Now, look, X,' said the CO, 'if I have those handcuffs removed, will you give me your word not to escape again?'

'Yes, sir,' said Private X simply.

I was impressed with his sincerity. If he had said: 'May I be struck dead if I do,' I would have warned the CO that he was not to be trusted, but his quiet 'Yes, sir,' suggested to me, with all my knowledge and experience of witnesses, that he meant it. I said as much to the CO.

'All right,' said the CO. 'They can take off the handcuffs.'

They took them off, and a few days later Private X left our battalion – not under escort – but under his own steam and, as far as I know, he was never heard of again.

Somehow or other I survived that episode, and actually became adjutant. A few months later, when the CO was on leave, a man was brought up on a charge before the acting CO, who relied implicitly on me as adjutant to steer him safely through the legal channels. It was a bad case and he sent the man to detention. After he had been taken away, a horrible thought occurred to me.

'I'm afraid there's been a slip-up,' I said. 'You ought to have asked him if he'd take your award or have a court martial.'

The acting CO said (I thought very moderately): 'You might have told me. What do we do now?'

'Better have him back and ask him.'

We had him back.

'Private Y,' said the acting CO, 'I ought to have asked you whether you'd take my award or have a court martial.'

Private Y thought for a moment.

'I'll have a court martial, sir,' he said.

There was a pause. The acting CO looked at me. I looked straight in front of me. Eventually the prisoner was marched out.

'Now what?' asked the acting CO.

'We're in a mess,' I said. 'If he's court-martialled he can say he's already been tried by you, and a man can't be tried twice for the same offence. If you send him to do his sentence, he can complain that it's illegal, as he was never given the chance of a court martial.'

'Well, what do we do?'

'The only thing to do is for me to see him and to try to persuade him to accept your award.'

'But he says he won't.'

'I know, but, if we can tell him that you won't send him to detention and will only give him CB, he might agree.'

'But he ought to get detention for this,' said the acting CO.

'And so ought you, if I may say so,' he added.

'I'm very sorry,' I said, 'but there's nothing else to be done.'

'All right. Better go along and see him.'

So the sergeant-major and I visited Private Y.

'Private Y,' I said, 'supposing the CO were to reconsider your punishment, d'you think you'd accept his award then?'

'That depends, sir, don't it?' said Private Y.

'Depends on what?' I said, though I knew very well what he meant.

'On wot the award's going to be,' said Private Y. 'I ain't unreasonable, sir,' he added. 'If you'll tell me, I'll tell you.'

'Well,' I said, as airily as I could, 'undoubtedly a slight mistake has been made and I think it possible that in the circumstances the CO might substitute an award of CB. But, of course, I can't bind him in any way.'

'But he knows you've come to see me, don't he, sir?' said Private Y.

'Well, yes, he does.'

'And 'e knows what you were going to say to me, sir?' he asked.

It occurred to me that Private Y might have done very well at the Bar himself. After he had most respectfully cross-examined me a little further he agreed to accept the CO's award. So he was duly marched in again, asked the missing question and given a trifling punishment of 5 days' CB. He saluted very smartly next time I saw him in the battalion lines.

Well, everyone can make mistakes and I lived down that one too. I forget how long it was after this that an unpleasant situation arose in one of the companies. Someone was stealing.

They knew who it was but they couldn't prove anything. He was too fly, they said.

'Too fly,' I said to myself. 'We'll see who's too fly.' I spoke to his Company Commander.

'Don't worry,' I said. 'You lend him to battalion headquarters. Then we'll set a trap for him. I know all about these things.'

So Private Z was duly transferred to battalion headquarters. I decided to give him a couple of days to allay any possible suspicion and then to set some simple trap. Everyone hates a chap who steals from his comrades, and I had no compunction about it. But I knew that sometimes traps fail for lack of efficiency. There would be nothing like that in this case. I would go into it personally. I knew the dangers and there would be no mistakes. Unfortunately, however, on the very night that Private Z first slept at battalion headquarters the battalion safe was broken open and all the money taken. I at once arranged for at least a dozen men, including Private Z, to have their kits thoroughly inspected and searched, but nothing traceable to the robbery was found.

'I had nothing to do with the safe business, sir,' volunteered Private Z. 'Why should you think I had?'

The question itself was almost a confession of guilt. No one had said a word to him about the safe.

'Everyone's being searched,' I said.

'Oh no they aren't, sir. Only me and them.'

'Well, there are twelve of you.'

'But why pick on me, sir? I ain't done nothing. I've only just come here. I didn't even know where the safe was. Anyway, what should I want to break it open for?'

Everything he said was the hallmark of the thief, and he was obviously the guilty party, but we couldn't prove a thing against him. I sent him back to his Company at once with many thanks for the loan.

'I told you he was too fly,' said his Company Commander, 'even for you.'

I got my CO to send me on an assault course. There's no law about that. You just break your neck or get shot.

The Application

Mr Justice Frinstead sat in Death's waiting-room, looking at but not reading one of the many magazines provided for the use of customers. It was a copy of the Law Journal, opened at a page which contained an article referring to one of his recent judgments. Like most customers in this particular waiting-room, however, he was not really in a condition to take in the printed words. He was thinking too much of the interview which lay before him. The atmosphere in the ante-room of Death is even less conducive to reading than that in a doctor's or dentist's, though ample material is provided for those who want it. Most people do what Mr Justice Frinstead was doing: they put a magazine in front of them and don't read it.

He was one of the senior High Court judges and, as such, he had often had to deal with applications by litigants for postponements of their cases. They were made on various grounds, though in most instances, whatever the ground put forward, the real reason for the application was, in the judge's belief, the fact that the solicitors on one side or the other had not sufficiently prepared their cases. He was often right, though not quite as often as he thought. Even when he was right, however, you might have thought that an adjournment would be granted in such cases so that the litigant should not be unnecessarily prejudiced by his solicitor's carelessness.

But Mr Justice Frinstead thought very differently. Every experienced practitioner at the Bar knew that, if he wished to make a successful application for an adjournment before that particular judge, he would have to work very hard for it, and that it would be fatal to admit that the parties were not ready for trial. It is, of course, necessary that the lists of cases should not be allowed to get into disorder by too many applications for adjournments. As, however, solicitors are officers of the Court, there should be little difficulty in making them behave themselves properly without prejudicing the litigants, who, after all, are the people to be mainly considered in Courts of Justice. Of course, in a genuine case of illness, an adjournment could usually be obtained. Even then, however, the nature of the illness and its probable duration would be carefully scrutinised, and Mr Justice Frinstead would give the impression that he thought it somewhat contemptuous of anyone to be ill when he had a case in the list.

Sometimes the real reason for the application for an adjournment was that counsel was engaged in another case. It might in some instances be very prejudicial for the litigant to change horses in midstream, but it was no use saying anything like this to Mr Justice Frinstead. If you were unwise enough to do so, he would merely congratulate you on being so busy and refuse the application. It was, in fact, this judge's normal practice in refusing these applications (which he seemed to do with alacrity and some unexplained pleasure) to indulge in some heavy sarcasm, which would sometimes produce titters from those who were not at the moment affected by it.

As Mr Justice Frinstead sat in the waiting-room, many thoughts raced through his mind, but the most important of these was that he would like to live a little longer. As he was considering regretfully the many delights which life yet held for him, the door of the waiting-room opened and Death walked in and asked if he was ready. Almost instinctively the judge said: 'Would it be possible, my Lord, to apply for a short adjournment?'

'On what grounds?'

'Quite frankly, my Lord, I am not yet ready.'

'Not ready, Sir George? Surely you have had enough warning? Your case has been in my list for months, not to say for years.'

'I must admit, my Lord, that I have known that I have had a weak heart for a long time and that this might happen to me, but, now that it has happened, it seems so terribly sudden.'

'Shouldn't you have thought of that before, Sir George? I seem to recollect that in similar applications made to you that is the sort of answer you have given the applicant.'

'Perhaps I was wrong sometimes, my Lord.'

'That may well be, Sir George. But is it not rather late to have discovered that? What redress have the unfortunate litigants whose applications for postponements were refused?'

Death paused, but the judge said nothing.

'I gather from your silence,' Death went on, 'that you have no answer to that. Well, then, what other grounds have you for this adjournment of your case?'

'Quite frankly, my Lord, I enjoy my life and would like some more of it.'

'That is an unusually honest answer, Sir George. D'you think that, if I grant your application, you might in the future be more ready to grant other people's?'

'Oh, my Lord, I feel sure of it.'

'Well, Sir George, in view of the frankness which you have shown in making your application and, in particular, in view of the fact that you have candidly admitted that there are no grounds whatever for my granting it, I will postpone the hearing of your case for the moment. You may go. Good morning.'

As in a dream, Mr Justice Frinstead bowed himself out and gradually came back through unconsciousness to life and, after a lengthy period of convalescence, to his duties. Shortly after his return to work, he was about to hear applications for adjournments. Suddenly a young member of the Bar, wholly inexperienced in these matters (and, indeed, in almost every other matter connected with the practice of the law), out of his turn (because it is customary for such applications to be made in order of seniority) leapt to his feet and, in a very young man's voice, loud and clear, asked to be allowed to mention the case of Brown v Smith. The judge looked along the row of more senior barristers waiting to make their applications and, pausing only to remark: 'There seems to be a dearth of applications this morning,' gave the young man leave to mention Brown v Smith.

'My Lord, in that case I have an application that it should stand out of the list for one month.'

'Upon what grounds?'

'The best possible grounds, my Lord; the case is not ready for trial.'

The more senior members of the Bar waited, smiling like schoolboys, for the storm to break.

Mr Justice Frinstead licked his lips. But, just as he was about to reduce the young man to a state of stuttering confusion, he suddenly remembered his own application for an adjournment and the reprieve which frankness had brought him.

'Well, Mr – Mr …' (he looked at the slip of paper containing the young man's name) … 'Mr Forsyth, it is certainly refreshing to have to consider such an honest application.'

The Bar looked puzzled but assumed that heavy sarcasm was about to be brought into play. They never learned how wrong they were. The judge had every intention of granting the young man's application. Suddenly, however, he felt a dreadful pain tearing at his heart and he just had time to reverse his intention and to refuse the application before he died.

I Forget the Name

'I'll forget my own name next,' said the speaker. 'Not likely I won't,' he added. 'But you will, madam. And you. And you. And you.' He pointed to various members of his audience. 'How many times have *you* said that, *and* meant it? Just think. More than you'd care to say. And you don't like to put it down to old age creeping on, because that's too near the truth. Like necks. Faces can lie, but not necks. Look at a horse's teeth and a woman's neck. But this isn't a beauty parlour. I can't rejuvenate you. Nor, if you want to know, can anyone else. Youth comes from within. It's in here or up here,' and he pointed to his heart and his head. 'There, ladies and gentlemen. Not out of a pot or a tube or a bottle or in the fat hands of a masseuse – or worse, a masseur.'

There's no doubt about it. Archie could talk. And the meetings he had organised were a considerable success. But Archie could not only talk. He had ideas, and knew how to use them. That is, when he was after the money. Which was always. And they were simple ideas. Ideas which made everyone say: 'Why didn't *I* think of that?' Like cats'-eyes on the road. It'll be white lines next. Archie often thought what a waste of labour it is for all those men week after week to have to paint them again. Surely there's something more permanent than a white line. Something to last a year or so, anyway. There's a fortune for someone round the corner.

It was forgetting the name of a horse that first gave Archie the idea. He was wild. It was only a few minutes before the 'off'. Sometimes one hasn't the money for the call, but he'd got that all right. First he forgot the bookie's number. But he could look that up – and did. And then, as soon as the girl answered, the name of the horse went right out of his head. And it wasn't as though he'd only heard of it that day. He'd been backing it for weeks. And it always lost. But, once he'd started, he couldn't stop. He had to be on it every time. And then came the day when Archie woke in the morning and felt sure it was going to win. He worked out what he'd lost and decided to put on enough to give him a profit. And there he was, on the blower.

'Be quick, please,' said the bookie's young lady. 'They'll be off in a minute.'

'Just a moment,' said Archie. 'It's on the tip of my tongue. I've got it. No I haven't. I'll forget my own name next. Look, Miss, would you mind reading out the runners?'

'OK,' she said, and began.

She'd got halfway when: 'Sorry,' she said, 'they're off. Would you like to hold for the result?'

Archie held on, knowing what was coming. Never had he prayed so heartily for a horse to lose. But he knew it wouldn't. If ever there was a racing certainty, this was it. He could have thrown the receiver through the window when she told him the result. And it was ten to one.

But Archie was not one for sitting down under misfortune. He began to think of the number of people he'd met who'd had the same sort of experience. And of people who couldn't think of an old friend's name when they were out with another one and met her. Everyone suffered from it. Why couldn't he provide a cure? Or, next best thing, why couldn't he persuade people that he'd got a cure? And so the idea was born.

He only advertised in a small way to begin with. But, as the idea caught on, he grew bolder. And the customers rolled up. He didn't offer them the world. He didn't say he could improve their memory as a whole. 'Just names,' he said, 'that's all. I'll help you to remember names. Money back if not satisfied.'

His plan, like his idea, was simple. He went to the library and looked up a few medical books, and then made a simple electrical apparatus with a few attractive red lights. And this is how it worked.

'I go to a lot of parties,' a customer would say, 'and I simply can't remember the names of people I'm introduced to. But, worse than that, when I give a party I can't remember the names of my guests. I write them down beforehand, and try so hard. But, as soon as they arrive, all my preparations are wasted.'

'I know,' Archie would say, 'and then you have to make silly clucking noises to try and pretend you're saying the names. "This is Mr Hochloch – Mrs Werewish." If you say that sort of thing quietly and quickly, you hope it will pass as a name. Sometimes it does, but not with Americans. They say: "I didn't quite catch the name. What is it, please?" and, unless it's volunteered at once, you're sunk and have to confess. And even with English people, if you've said "Mr Hochloch", you look awfully silly when he says his name is Brandon-Peabody.'

'You're absolutely right. But how can I be cured?'

'Quite simply, madam. The brain, as you probably know, is divided into several parts. Running along underneath the temples is what we call the temporal lobes of the brain. You've two of them. One on each side. They contain the memory. It is there that Mr Brandon-Peabody's name lives in your mind. But he's buried too deep. So, when you want him, you can't find him. How to bring him to the surface, that's the problem. And I supply the answer.'

'And that is?'

'I'll tell you. Some unfortunate people are given drugs, or even have an operation on the brain, to make them forget. They are given something to depress the temporal lobes. Something to drive away the name of Mr Brandon-Peabody – who may, for example, have assaulted you in the park – nothing personal, madam, just by way of explanation – you need something to erase the name of Brandon-Peabody – or, if you cannot cut him out altogether, to drive him deep down. Down, down, down, so that the memory of that terrible afternoon will haunt you no longer. Right. No doubt you've heard of that sort of thing. Now, just as the temporal lobes – the memory – can be depressed, so they can be stimulated. What's my name, madam?' he suddenly interjected.

'Your name? Your name? I've forgotten.'

'Exactly. Not buried as deep as Mr Brandon-Peabody, I hope, and certainly not for the same reason – there's no need to move, madam – but too deep down to be recovered in a moment. And, don't forget, it's only a moment you have. No use remembering the Dowager Duchess of Longchamp's name when she's well past the saluting base. Now, the problem is to stimulate the temporal lobes without the use of harmful drugs. And the solution is here.'

And he points to the machine.

'Do I have to put on that thing that looks like a hairdryer?'

'You do.'

'And do I feel anything?'

'Not a thing, madam, not a thing.'

'And what happens?'

'We pass an almost imperceptible amount of electric current through the temporal lobes, and they are stimulated. And Mr Brandon-Peabody's name is pushed up to the surface.'

'But, if it works, why hasn't anyone done it before?'

'Why not indeed? Why didn't anyone invent anaesthetics three hundred years ago? Or Penicillin fifty years ago? Why not? You may well ask, madam. Much as I respect the medical profession, if I may say so, madam, their inventive powers move more like steam-rollers than racing cars. The truth is, madam, that we progress all the time and someone has to be the first. Now, madam, if you will allow me.'

He puts the contraption on the lady's head, presses a switch and a red light shines. Then it blinks once or twice and he turns it off.

'That's all it is, madam.'

He removes the contraption.

'You'll find an immediate improvement after this one treatment. What's my name, madam?'

'Mr Thompson.'

Archie's surname – Thompson – was in quite large letters on the machine.

'Thank you, madam. You couldn't do that five minutes ago. With another five treatments you will find that, not only will you have no problems with the Duchess of Longchamp or Mr Brandon-Peabody, but all the Brownes and Smythes, with or without an "e", will be supplied readily by your stimulated temporal lobes. And, if in a year or so you require a refresher course, you know where to come.'

What was the reason for Archie's success? The electric current was no more than was necessary to light a small pocket torch and could have no possible effect whatever – apart from the fact that it didn't go through the temporal or any other lobes at all. It is perfectly true that a few people asked for their money back. And, of course, they got it. But they were only a few. And why? Quite simple. The failure to be able to introduce people whose names you know quite well is almost entirely due to lack of confidence. It is the fear of forgetting their names momentarily that in fact induces you to forget them. So that all Archie had to do to succeed was to instil confidence in his clients. An electric appliance with a flashing red light and a lot of talk can work wonders, and it did.

His fame began to spread and he did very nicely. The expenditure in 1/4-volt batteries was negligible and the total of the fees was not. One day a prosperous-looking man came to Archie's premises and said he'd like to make a few enquiries about the machine before he risked it.

'Of course. That's what we expect,' said Archie.

The man hesitated for a moment, and then said: 'Haven't I seen you somewhere before?'

One can always imagine one has seen a person before if one tries, and for a moment Archie did begin to think it wasn't their first meeting – but he couldn't place the man at all.

'It's possible,' he said, 'but I can't be sure.'

'Never mind,' replied the man. 'Now, tell me about it.'

Archie gave him the usual jargon. When he had finished, the man said: 'D'you guarantee it won't hurt in any way?'

'In writing, if you wish.'

'Yes,' said the man, 'I would like it in writing.'

'With pleasure,' said Archie, and handed him a form of guarantee which he'd drawn up for suspicious customers.

'In spite of the fact that it stimulates the temporal lobes?'

'Guaranteed,' said Archie.

'All right,' said the man, 'I'll try it. How much d'you say it is?'

At that time it was a guinea per treatment, and Archie said so.

'Right,' said the man, 'off we go.'

Archie fixed on the head-dress and switched on and then off. On and off. On and off. He'd found that it was more impressive if it lasted longer.

Eventually: 'It's all over,' said Archie, and took off the head-dress. 'Feel all right, sir?'

'Perfect.'

'Just as I said.'

'Just as you said. I congratulate you,' went on the man. 'No pain, and it's worked already. I remember who you are now. The last time I saw you was at the Old Bailey. You'd just got two years for a confidence trick.'

Archie said nothing.

'I'm Detective-Inspector Scarborough. D'you want to make a statement?'

'Very well,' said Archie. There seemed no point in doing anything else.

'Right,' said the inspector, and got out his notebook. He was about to write when suddenly he paused. 'Good Lord,' he said, 'I know the face, but I've forgotten the name.'

The Patient

Miss Coombe was exceptionally attractive and efficient and she had a very good memory. Most important thing, memory, for a secretary and an admirable secretary she was, particularly for Lionel Parsons (formerly Smith), a dentist who was trying hard to acquire a West End practice.

He had had rather bad luck. Qualified not long before the war, he had served with the forces and, on demobilisation, had started ambitiously in Harley Street. He had made a good beginning when a patient claimed damages against him for negligence. He denied liability. In consequence a solicitor's letter was followed by a writ, and eventually the case was heard before Mr Justice Pantin. Rather foolishly Mr Smith (as he then was) treated the matter too lightly and was facetious in the witness-box. This is a dangerous line to take, particularly if your case is not cast-iron. You may score a point or two over counsel, but there is not much value in that, if you lose the case.

Part of the defendant Smith's cross-examination by a rather pompous QC went as follows:

QC: Now, Mr Smith, was the plaintiff in pain when he came to you?

Defendant: Yes, he was.

QC: To what did you attribute the pain?

Defendant: That something was wrong with a tooth.

QC: Really, Mr Smith, this is no laughing matter. You might just as well have said that he had toothache.

Defendant: I nearly did.

QC: Really, sir, you may not find this is so amusing when the case is over.

Defendant: I don't find it amusing at all. But you asked me what I thought was wrong with a patient who was in pain and came to see me. I'm a dentist and I assumed it was toothache.

QC: Would you do me the courtesy of attending to my question, sir? I did not ask you what you thought was wrong with him. I said – and I repeat – to what did you attribute the pain?

Defendant: And I still say toothache.

Judge: Mr Smith, the plaintiff's counsel wants you to be a little more specific. He's not referring to the moment your patient came into the room. He wants to know what conclusions you came to about the pain after you had examined him. What was the cause of the pain? Decay in a tooth, or what?

Defendant: I see, my Lord. Then why didn't he say so in the first instance?

QC: Because I thought you could understand plain English, sir.

Defendant: I can – if it isn't spoken too fast.

Judge: Now, Mr Smith, don't be pert.

Defendant: I'm sorry, my Lord.

QC: Thank you, my Lord. And now, sir, if you will be kind enough to attend to the question – and I will dot every *i* and cross every *t* for your benefit – after you had first examined the patient to what cause did you attribute the pain?

Defendant: You want that exact question answered?

QC: I do, sir, if it is not troubling you too much.

Defendant: Not at all. I attributed the pain to something being wrong with a tooth.

QC: Really, sir, this is too bad. No one imagines that it was due to a bad toe or a sore ear.

Defendant: Toe, no, sir, but you're on more dangerous ground with the ear. Have you ever heard of sympathetic pains?

QC: Don't ask me questions. We all know there was something wrong with the plaintiff's tooth. I want to know to what you attributed the pain.

Defendant: You said 'in the first instance'.

QC: Very well – what was it?

Defendant: That something was wrong with a tooth.

QC: If you think you are going to deflect me from my cross-examination by your behaviour, sir, you are very much mistaken.

Defendant: I'm sure that nothing could.

Judge: Now, Mr Smith, you mustn't be rude to counsel.

Defendant: I'm sorry, my Lord, but I wish he would make his questions clearer. When a dentist first examines a patient, he wants to ascertain, if he can, where the pain comes from. Patients sometimes complain of one tooth when it is in fact another which is causing the trouble. The first thing to do is to find out exactly where the patient thinks the pain is coming from. And that's what I did in the first instance. I discovered that the plaintiff was getting pain which appeared to come from a particular tooth. The probability was that that was the seat of the trouble but, without further examination, it was by no means certain.

Accordingly I answered counsel's question quite correctly by saying that my first examination disclosed that he had a pain in a tooth. Which tooth I did not know for certain though I had a good idea. The cause of the pain I did not know at all.

QC: I am very much obliged to you, Mr Smith.

Defendant: Not at all. Is that all you wish to ask?

QC: It is by no means all I wish to ask, and you know it.

Defendant: I do now.

QC: Tell me, sir, after you had examined the patient thoroughly – did you hear the word 'thoroughly', sir?

Defendant: I did.

QC: Do you know what it means?

Defendant: Thoroughly.

QC: Yes. Well, sir?

Defendant: Well – what?

QC: I asked if you knew what the word 'thoroughly' means.

Defendant: And I said I did.

QC: You did not.

Defendant: I did.

Judge: Really, gentlemen, this has gone far enough. I'm sure the witness knows what is meant by the word. Do let's get on with the case.

QC: If your Lordship pleases. After you had examined the patient thoroughly – and I shall assume that you understand the meaning of that word …

Defendant: Thoroughly.

QC: Don't interrupt me, sir. After such examination to what conclusion did you come as to the cause of the pain?

Defendant: May I ask a question?

QC: No, answer mine.

Judge: Just one moment. What is the question?

Defendant: Well – my Lord – I should like to know what counsel means by 'examine'.

Judge: That's a fair question.

QC: By 'examine', sir, I mean what you are paid to do. Examine the plaintiff's mouth – not his hands or his feet or his hair, but his mouth, sir.

Defendant: But how?

QC: I can well believe, sir, from your treatment of my client, that you do not know how to examine a patient – but it is not for me to teach you.

Judge: But what I think the witness means is whether you want his conclusions after merely looking at the plaintiff's mouth or after, perhaps, having drilled into the tooth.

Defendant: That's the point, my Lord.

QC: Well, after you had examined his mouth.

Defendant: What conclusion did I come to?

QC: Yes.

Defendant: None.

QC: None?

Defendant: None except …

QC: Go on, sir.

Defendant: … Well, I thought you'd prefer me not to.

QC: Why d'you think I'm cross-examining you, sir? To amuse myself, or you, sir? Kindly finish your answer. You came to no conclusion except …?

Defendant: That he had toothache.

QC: Pshaw!

Defendant: I told you you wouldn't like it.

Judge:	Mr Smith, it won't help you to be flippant.
QC:	Thank you, my Lord. If this witness treats his patients as flippantly as he treats me and the Court, I'm not surprised he has to face an action for negligence.
Judge:	Don't make speeches, please.
QC:	Very well, sir; after examining the patient you came to no conclusion as to the cause of the pain?
Defendant:	Except that it was probably in a tooth.
QC:	And what did you do then?
Defendant:	I made a further investigation.
QC:	With what results?
Defendant:	None.
QC:	Then what did you do?
Defendant:	What did I do?
QC:	Yes.
Defendant:	I took out the tooth.
QC:	You took out the tooth?
Defendant:	Yes.
QC:	Why?
Defendant:	Because he said it hurt him, and ...
QC:	Because he said it hurt him! You've already told me that he might have been wrong.
Defendant:	I'd like to finish the sentence, if I may.
QC:	Well, what do you want to add?
Defendant:	The patient asked me to take it out.
QC:	Aren't you the better judge of whether a tooth should come out or not? Or perhaps I should say oughtn't you to be the better judge?
Defendant:	Well, after all, it's his tooth, and he wanted it out. So I took it out.
QC:	Much less trouble than drilling the tooth and examining it, and perhaps stopping it?

Defendant: Much less painful, too.

QC: Now, sir, I was coming to that. Why was it much less painful?

Defendant: Because I gave him a local anaesthetic. I don't do that if I can help it with ordinary drilling.

QC: Why not, sir? D'you like to see your patients writhe?

Defendant: Not at all. But, unless one knows for certain what is wrong, the patient's reaction to pain is or may be very helpful. In my early days I once took out a wrong tooth because the patient couldn't feel any pain.

QC: And how much did you have to pay for that, sir?

Defendant: Nothing at all. As a matter of fact the patient was very pleased and decided to have the lot out. What happened in that case was ...

QC: I'm not interested in that case, sir.

Defendant: I'm sorry. You asked me about it.

QC: Now, sir, you gave my client a local anaesthetic. What precautions did you take to see if it was safe to give it to him?

Defendant: I asked him if he'd prefer gas, and he said no.

QC: Is that what you call a precaution?

Defendant: Certainly. I like to give a patient what he wants, if I can. That's a precaution against his complaining.

QC: Whether it's safe or not?

Defendant: Of course I thought it was safe.

QC: But it wasn't in this case, was it?

Defendant: As events have turned out, perhaps not.

QC: And that is because he had an abscess, is it not?

Defendant: Mainly, yes.

QC: Entirely, sir?

Defendant: It's impossible to say entirely. The bloodstream in every patient varies – and so does his reaction to poison. But I quite agree that the plaintiff's subsequent illness as mainly due to his being given a local anaesthetic when he had an abscess.

QC: Isn't it elementary that a dentist does not give a local anaesthetic when the patient has an abscess?

Defendant: Not usually.

QC: Then why did you give him one?

Defendant: I did not know he had an abscess.

QC: If you had examined him more carefully, you would have found it.

Defendant: If I'd opened up the tooth – yes, but he asked me to take it out.

QC: Are there no other means of ascertaining whether an abscess exists?

Defendant: X-ray or pressure on the gum may show it.

QC: Did you X-ray the tooth?

Defendant: No.

QC: Why not?

Defendant: I didn't think it was necessary. I'd have to X-ray every patient who wanted a tooth out at that rate. I don't know what the Health Service would say to that.

QC: What about pressure?

Defendant: I didn't notice anything to make me suspect an abscess.

QC: But there might have been one?

Defendant: There was one.

QC: Thank you.

Judge: It is well recognised, is it, that it may be dangerous to use local anaesthetics when an abscess is suspected?

Defendant: Yes, my Lord.

Judge: When you know the cause of the pain and that it is not an abscess, other things being equal, a local anaesthetic is quite safe?

Defendant: Yes, my Lord.

Judge: But when you don't know the cause of the pain and it might be due to an abscess, don't you think you ought to take further precautions before using a local anaesthetic?

Defendant: I will another time, my Lord.

Judge: Exactly. You see, I expect that in most cases you can trace the cause of the pain?

Defendant: Yes, my Lord.

Judge: Well, then, I don't see why the Health Service should object to the expense of X-ray in the infrequent cases where you don't know the cause of pain and where abscesses cannot be ruled out.

Defendant: I see what you mean, my Lord.

Judge: We know that abscesses couldn't be ruled out in this case. How long was the patient in your chair before you took out the tooth?

Defendant: About ten minutes, my Lord.

Judge: Don't you think that, looking back on the matter now, you acted rather hastily in using a local anaesthetic without knowing whether or not there was an abscess?

Defendant: Perhaps I did, my Lord.

Eventually the judge awarded £500 damages against him. He was insured against the financial loss but the resultant publicity was fatal. He changed his name to Parsons and started all over again. Just before the case, he had engaged Miss Coombe. This was a stroke of luck. There were few dentists who had nurse-secretaries like Miss Coombe, and quite a number of his male patients came as much to look at her as to be treated by him. After all, within certain limits, it doesn't make a great deal of difference who stops or takes out your teeth and, if there is a really charming girl to make the appointment and distract your attention during the torture, it is quite an advantage.

One evening at about five o'clock the telephone rang and Miss Coombe answered it.

'You won't know me, I'm afraid,' said a voice. 'I'm clerk to Mr Justice Robinson – Sir Charles Robinson.'

'Oh – yes?' said Miss Coombe, in her sweetest voice.

'I'm so very sorry to trouble you but I wonder if by any chance you'd be able to help Sir Charles. Mr Grant has mentioned Mr Parsons' name. Sir Charles is in considerable pain and his own dentist unfortunately can't see him or suggest a substitute. Is there any possibility of Mr Parsons' seeing him tonight?'

'Well,' said Miss Coombe meditatively, surveying the blank engagement book, 'he has a patient with him now and there's another at five-thirty, and then one at six. Let me see. Will you hold the line a moment, please?'

'Certainly,' said Mr Justice Robinson's clerk.

'A new patient,' whispered Miss Coombe to Mr Parsons, who was sitting in a chair doing a crossword puzzle.

'Good,' said Mr Parsons. 'Let's hope he wants dentures.'

'Are you there?' went on Miss Coombe into the telephone.

'Yes.'

'I'll tell you what I'll try to do. The six o'clock case isn't a very serious one and I'll see if I can put the patient off. If

Sir Charles could be here at six, Mr Parsons will try to see him then, but if the six o'clock patient does come I'm afraid Sir Charles will have to wait till about half past.'

'Oh, that will be quite all right,' said the clerk. 'Sir Charles will be very grateful to you.'

Miss Coombe with some pleasure told Mr Parsons who his new patient was.

'A High Court judge,' said Mr Parsons. 'That's a bit of luck. I wonder who he goes to in the normal way. I expect he'll stay with us once he's seen you.'

'Mr Parsons,' said Miss Coombe, 'if you say that once more I shall ask for a rise in salary.'

'If it happens once more, you shall have it.'

At six o'clock punctually the judge arrived. In spite of his pain he did not fail to notice the charm of Miss Coombe. She chatted with him for a few minutes and then took him into the surgery.

'It's extremely kind of you to see me,' said the judge. 'I can't tell you how grateful I am.'

Mr Parsons had never to his knowledge seen a judge out of Court before, and he looked at him curiously.

'Only too pleased to help. Now, let me see, what's the trouble?'

The judge sat in the chair and opened his mouth.

'Oh, yes, I see,' said Mr Parsons, after a short examination. 'Must be rather painful, I'm afraid.'

'It is a little.'

'When I was a small boy,' said Mr Parsons, 'my dentist had goldfish in front of the patient to distract his attention. People don't do that these days. D'you think it's a good idea?'

'I've really never considered it.'

'I should value your opinion, sir,' said Mr Parsons.

'I have no opinion. I have toothache.'

'Well, we'll see what we can do. A little wider, please. That's right. Thank you.'

Mr Parsons set to work and, after the manner of dentists, held a one-sided conversation with the judge.

'It must be a dreadful responsibility being a judge.' The judge could only look at the dentist. His eyes might have been saying 'Yes, it is' or 'No, it isn't' or 'Please don't talk but just get on with the job.'

'I've only been in Court once.'

The judge tried to look 'Indeed?'

'Yes, a case of my own. Close a little, please. Must say, if you'll forgive me, I don't think much of the law. I'm afraid this is going to hurt a little.'

'Ough,' said the judge.

'Sorry. I shan't be doing this very long.'

'Very long' is a comparative expression.

'No, it's all right – *you* didn't try it – I remember the name, Mr Justice Pantin. A little wider, please. I suppose he tried it quite fairly, really, but I imagine a man who loses a case often thinks he's had a hard deal.'

He allowed the judge to answer: 'I'm afraid that's bound to happen sometimes.'

'Oh well, I expect I've no right to grouse, but I must say that what I didn't like was the way I was cross-examined. I can't think why judges allow it these days. Serjeant Buzfuz isn't in it.'

As he said the last words, Mr Parsons noticed that Miss Coombe, whose presence was not required near the chair at that moment, had come quite close to him. He frowned at her slightly, motioning her to go away. Although she retreated, she was obviously trying to say something to him with her eyes. Mr Parsons ignored the signal, whatever it was.

'This chap who cross-examined me,' he went on, 'was an absolute bounder. Yes, I'm afraid this will hurt rather.'

'Ough,' said the judge.

'I'll be as quick as I can.'

'Quick' is also a comparative expression.

'Yes, he was infernally rude to me. Asked me questions that had nothing to do with the case and then wouldn't wait for the answers. Most unfair. A really nasty piece of work, if you ask me.'

At that moment, he felt a distinct kick from Miss Coombe, who had crept up near the chair again.

He stopped his work, turned round and glared.

'I shan't want you for the moment, Miss Coombe,' he said.

'I wonder if I could have one word with you, sir?' she said.

'Not now, Miss Coombe,' he replied, 'you can see I'm busy. Sir Charles is in pain.'

He was.

With a last mute appeal Miss Coombe gave up the struggle and Mr Parsons returned to the judge.

'There should be some limit to the way these barristers behave. Do you feel that?'

'Yes,' said the judge.

'Very much?'

'Yes.'

'Oh. I'm afraid I can't give you an injection. It looks as though you've some infection and I can't risk it. I shan't be very long now. A little wider, please. Try not to jerk your head. I'm sorry it's so very painful. I should have liked to have been able to ask that QC some questions. The ridiculous things he asked me. Didn't really know the first thing about the case. Yet, whenever I tried to ask him anything, the judge stopped me. "You're there to answer questions, not ask them," he said. Does that hurt?'

'Yes,' said the judge. 'And another thing, I wish you wouldn't ask me questions when you're holding my mouth open. All you dentists do it. You must know we can't answer.'

'Most of us are married, I expect, sir, and it's a great thing to have the chance of speaking without interruption.'

'Well, I wish you wouldn't do it.'

'Another thing, sir,' said Mr Parsons, 'it helps to take the patient's mind off the pain.'

'Well, it is no help at all to me,' replied the judge.

'Very well, sir,' said Mr Parsons, 'I'll try to remember.'

The treatment went on for another quarter of an hour and, at last, Mr Justice Robinson, wet through as the result of his agonies, left the surgery after thanking Mr Parsons – perhaps a little more perfunctorily than when he came in – for seeing him at such short notice.

As soon as he had gone, Miss Coombe turned on Mr Parsons.

'Now you really have done it,' she said. 'You'll never see *him* again. D'you know who that was? I knew his face as soon as he came in, but I never knew his name. I tried to warn you. That was the QC who cross-examined you. He's a judge now.'

'So I believe,' said Mr Parsons, as he started to put away some of his instruments.

The Good-in-Man

It was just plain beastly. I had walked into the private bar of the Good-in-Man, and, if I had not been so thirsty, I think I should have walked straight out. I might have been prevented, though, by a desire to know what kind of person was responsible for the place. I waited a moment or two in the empty bar and then, in response to my knocking on the counter with a coin, he came in.

'Good afternoon, sir. What is it to be?'

'A pint of bitter, please.'

'And very nice too. A pint of bitter it is.' And he drew me a pint and handed it to me. I would not have cared for his type of familiarity in any event, but, in those surroundings, it seemed even more out of place. As I raised my tankard he spoke again.

'Your very good health, sir.'

I am a mild-mannered person and said: 'Thank you', but the fellow was starting to annoy me. His cheerful attitude, with those things all around, was provocative.

'Down she goes,' he said. 'That's better, isn't it?'

'Yes,' I said.

'The finest beer in England.'

'Oh,' I said.

'Very monosyllabic we are today,' he went on chirpily. 'Anything biting you? It's the decorations, I suppose.'

'Partly,' I said.

82

'Combination of me and them, I imagine?'

'Exactly,' I said.

'Three syllables,' he said cheerfully. 'You're coming on. We'll have a whole sentence out of you yet.'

'Do you usually talk to customers like this?'

'Well done,' he said. 'I knew it would come.' There was a pause. 'Have another go,' he said. I said nothing, and he went on: 'I suppose you want to know what it's all about, eh?' I still said nothing. 'Come on,' he said: 'No harm in saying what you think. Much better in fact. Ever so much better. Now what d'you think it's all in aid of?'

I dislike being rude to people and avoid scenes at almost any cost. Consequently, if the fellow hadn't gone on, I should not have dreamed of saying what I thought about him or his bar. But now he really was asking for it. And, after a moment's hesitation, I decided to let him have it. But first I prepared the ground so that he could have no reason for complaint.

'Do you really want to know what I think?'

'Of course. That's what I've been asking. Fire ahead.' He put his elbows on the bar and his head between his hands and gazed at me intently. As I didn't immediately begin, he goaded me with: 'Three, two, one – gun.'

'You are obviously,' I eventually said, slowly and deliberately, 'an exhibitionist of a peculiarly nasty sort, with a loathing for mankind.' I stopped, and he still gazed at me intently.

'Go on,' he said. 'Finish it. Add pepper and salt to taste.'

'That will do for the moment,' I said.

'Oh, very well, I suppose I shall have to make do with that. Will you have another pint before I explain?'

I gave him my tankard.

'Shall I have one with you?'

'That's up to you,' I said.

'Now, that's very civil of you,' he said. 'I don't mind if I do. I'll have a whisky.' He poured out the drinks. 'That'll be seven-and-four. Hope you don't mind. I had a double. There's no hurry. You can cash up later. Now, where shall I begin?'

The fellow's impudence was starting to fascinate me, but not the things round the wall. Almost every part of it was taken up with a photograph or picture of some disaster. Shipwreck, flood, fire, famine, war scenes of all kinds – all the things of which one hates to be reminded. Some of the scenes were heartrending, some brutal, and the general concentrated effect of all of them was almost beyond description. Beastly was a mild word.

'Exhibitionist? Yes,' he said. 'I plead guilty to that. Who isn't in one way or another? But – a loathing for mankind? Not on your life. Just the opposite. I love my fellow man. I wish he were better, of course, but I love the good in him that there is.'

'You've a funny way of showing it.'

'Have I? You noticed the name of this pub?'

'I did. I'm surprised you haven't changed it.'

'I have. It was the Red Cow when I bought it. The Good-in-Man is my own invention.' He paused. Then, 'Go on, snort louder. I could hardly hear it,' he said. 'Now look,' he added, 'you see this glass which looks as though it contains whisky – the drink you were good enough to buy me.'

'I see it.'

'Well – I dare say you know there's pretty well no whisky about it. My drink's in the till – or will be when you cash up. Pretty mean? All landlords do it. They have to. But I agree it isn't a nice practice. Then again, how did I get this drink out of you? By a trick. That was mean, if you like. So here I am, a mean little man. You'll agree to that, I expect.'

'You should know,' I said.

'Now, supposing there were a car accident outside and they brought the bodies in here – some hurt – some just shaken. What would I do then? There'd be drinks all round on the house. I dare say it might kill some of them. As you know, there are times when brandy's the worst thing. But I'm not a doctor and don't know. So it wouldn't be my fault. But d'you see what I'm getting at? Everything at peace, no crisis, one solitary customer and I'm a mean little man, squeezing all I can get out of you. A crisis – and I give everything away cheerfully. Now, that's not just me – that's your man in the street. He's at his worst when times are normal, at his best when there's danger or destruction all round him. Now d'you see why I like these pictures? I like to be reminded of him at his best. Good heavens, there's enough tragedy and misery every day without these things round the walls – men and women and children dying before their time – from disease of one kind and another. Many more orphans through what one may call the normal channels than through this kind of thing. But, while proportionately there is only a minute amount of extra misery at a time of war or disaster, there is a fantastic amount of extra good. Then you see man at his most sublime. Look at that captain there. Probably as brutal as most captains of his time. Had men flogged to death and thought nothing of it. But there he is, going to his death without a murmur, while many of his crew are being saved. It's a fine picture, isn't it? That was his supreme moment. When I hear the silly little farmers squealing about the price of wheat and the labour and housing shortage, I like to remind myself that most of them would go down with their ships, if necessary. Still think I loathe my fellow men?'

I was puzzled. 'I'm beginning to see your point of view,' I said.

'Splendid,' he said. 'Drink that up and I'll tell you some more. Same again? Right. It's very good of you, I'm sure. No, don't bother to pay now. I'll chalk it up. I'll probably add it up wrong – in my own favour, of course, and after your sixth pint you won't notice. But these are the piping times of peace. That's what you must expect. Of course, if the house caught fire, it would be different. But I'm hoping it won't. Here's to you.'

I had now resigned myself to listening. I was in no hurry and it was a new experience.

'Now, where was I?' he went on. 'Oh – yes. We're all the same really. No offence, I hope, but you're the same as me. Look, suppose a chap had just left the bar and, after he'd gone, I said to you: "That chap's just done three years. Like to know his story?" You'd say, "Yes", wouldn't you – instead of letting the poor chap live it down. Well, I will tell you a story anyway. About a burglar. I expect you'd like to hear about him. Everyone likes to hear about burglars. Murderers more, of course, but a burglar will always do. I take it you're no exception?'

'Go on,' I said.

'Well, this one lived on the East Coast. That is to say he lived there when he wasn't in prison. Which wasn't often. He wasn't good at his job and they usually caught him after he'd been out a month or two. Of course, he was found work by the Discharged Prisoners Aid Society from time to time, but he couldn't stick regular work, and, like most criminals, he always thought he wouldn't be caught next time. He was usually described as a lazy good-for-nothing rascal, who was a public nuisance.

'Well, he got caught in the floods on the East Coast in 1953. And what does he do? Spends all his time rescuing people and animals. Day and night he worked. Pretty well exhausted himself physically. Mentally there wasn't much to exhaust. So this chap, who couldn't do an honest day's labouring, works forty-eight hours non-stop for nothing. Well, that isn't perhaps so surprising. Burglars have often made good soldiers. And there was a war on this time – against the floods.

'But this is the queer thing. When he'd done all he could, he went off towards the dry land. And, on his way, he passed house after house and cottage after cottage, all deserted, which he could have looted to his heart's content. The police did what they could, but they couldn't be everywhere and our burglar friend could have had the time of his life. *He didn't touch a thing.* But, as soon as he got into normal country, he chose a likely house and up the drainpipe he went. He slipped as he got through the window and woke the household. The householder had a revolver and a strong aversion to burglars.

' "You filthy little rat," he said. "Don't you move or I'll shoot. I mean it."

' "It's a fair cop, guv," said our friend, and, in due course, he finds his way to Quarter Sessions. There he is addressed by the Chairman.

' "You are a pest to society. Your record is a terrible one. It's obvious that you've never done a decent day's work in your life. You never have been any good and you never will be," and he goes down for twelve years. He never thought of mentioning what he'd done in the flood country. Not that it would have made any difference. He *was* a pest to society and the Chairman was quite right to put him away for years. But I like to remember not only what he did but what he *didn't* do in the floods. And I've got that photograph up there to remind me. Does this bore you? Or would you like some more?'

'Go on, please,' I said. 'But another pint first, and whatever you're having.'

'Thanks very much. Glad you've got into the swing of things so quickly. Here we go.'

We drank and he went on: 'My next example involves the eternal triangle – yes, the usual one, the husband George, the lover (he was called George too) and the wife Clarissa. The husband George was a good chap. He trusted his wife implicitly. The lover George hadn't *all* the vices but he was selfish and unscrupulous. He was a friend of George the husband, but, nevertheless, he did nothing to resist the temptation provided by Clarissa. On the contrary, he yielded to it and was soon determined to steal Clarissa from George the husband as soon as he could. But there was a difficulty. Lack of money. Clarissa liked the good things of life. George the husband could provide them. George the lover could not. Clarissa would have been quite happy to live with either George; indeed, she made the best of living with both Georges, but she did find it rather unsettling. And she found the necessary subterfuges rather a nuisance. And it was so easy to make a mistake. Every now and then she had to try and explain a remark which she accidentally made to George the husband instead of to George the lover. It was sometimes difficult to remember with whom an incident had occurred.

'Once she said to George the husband: "Oh – you've had that mole removed," before she remembered that it was on George the lover's back. George the husband was not in the least suspicious, or, if he was, he did not show it and seemed delighted if, when he went away on business, he knew that Clarissa would be entertained by George the lover. But the time came when Clarissa began to say to George the lover: "You really must make some money and take me away, or go away yourself. George will live for years and I'm getting bored with all this deceit. It must be one thing or the other."

' "But I love you," said George the lover.

' "Yes – yes," said Clarissa, "we all know that."

' "Not George, I hope?"

' "Well – he will do if you don't do something about it. I shall tell him myself and he'll kick you out. I'll give you a month."

'A week later they all went up to stay in the Lake District, and one day the two Georges went climbing together. They got caught in a freak storm, George the husband broke his ankle and they were out all night. As they'd changed their minds about the mountain they were going to climb after leaving the hotel, the search party which tried to find them had no success. The bad weather continued, then came fog and they had another night out. The cold and lack of food began to tell. Unless they could get back that day they would almost certainly die. George the lover might have got back by himself, but the prospect of trying to get George the husband back with him was more than formidable. It did just for a moment occur to George the lover to give George the husband a friendly push over the side when he wasn't looking and then to go back home for help, but he dismissed this unworthy thought immediately. Instead, he did in fact, by dint of the most tremendous exertion and great luck, eventually bring George the husband to safety. And so there was Clarissa, with her two Georges again. It's true that George the lover did, as I have said, think for a split second of making Clarissa a wealthy widow and marrying her soon afterwards, but, in fact, all he did was to save her husband at the risk of his own life. I keep that picture – "Cutting the rope" –

to remind me. Your tankard should be empty and my glass is about to be. Now that really is most kind of you.'

'Next gentleman, please,' I said.

'I'm glad the beer suits you. As I said, it's the best in England.'

'It certainly goes well with your stories.'

'It usually does. I think I'll tell you next about Mr Thompson, the clerk with the invisible ink. He had a most ingenious system for robbing his employer and had for years succeeded in avoiding detection. I won't tell you the details of his methods because, although I'm sure it wouldn't put ideas into your head, you might tell someone else who was less scrupulous. Anyway, the auditors never discovered a thing and, after seven years, Mr Thompson had succeeded in putting away a nice little pile. Though it had a large turnover, it was a one-man business and had no pension scheme for its employees. So Mr Thompson had made his own, with the assistance of his little bottle of invisible ink. When I say invisible, it looked like ordinary ink when you first used it, but in half-an-hour it had disappeared.

'Well, one day Mr Thompson's employer came into the office in an obviously troubled frame of mind. It was his wife. She was terribly ill. Nothing physical. Psychological. A trip round the world – at least six months – with her husband – was prescribed. Now Mr Thompson's employer couldn't afford to take the money out of the business and he hadn't sufficient savings to find the fare and keep his business going too. What happens? Mr Thompson advances his employer the money out of his savings – well everyone thought they were his own. Off goes the employer round the world and during the whole period of his absence, Mr Thompson never once uses his little bottle of invisible ink. Eventually the employer returns with his wife. She's been completely cured and the employer is a happy man.

'He's even happier when he finds the profits which the business has made during his absence. He raises Mr Thompson's salary, thanks him most warmly, starts repaying the loan by monthly instalments, and gives Mr Thompson a handsome present in addition. Mr Thompson expresses his pleasure at the recovery of his wife, waves aside the grateful thanks – "It's nothing at all, I assure you. I was only too pleased" – accepts the present, and then, once more, gets out his little bottle of invisible ink.

'Of course, you can say that he only did it to avoid killing the goose which laid the golden eggs, but I'm quite sure it wasn't that. The crisis came and Mr Thompson, like the ordinary man that he was, responded automatically to the call within him. The crisis over, Mr Thompson, like the ordinary man, returned to his normal mode of living. In his case it was crime; in other cases it's greed, arrogance, selfishness, laziness or what you will. Which reminds me, you're ready for another. And so am I.'

'I think I've time for one more,' I said.

'Good. Well, perhaps I'd better add up your bill – in case you leave in a hurry. No suggestions, I assure you, but accidents do happen, you know.'

I handed him some money and he handed me some change. I have no idea whether he cheated me or not.

'You're very trusting,' he said. 'You didn't count your change.'

'There was no point,' I replied. 'I don't know what the price of beer or whisky is in this house. I imagine it's a special price – except, of course, in an earthquake. And, in the circumstances, I must say I prefer to pay the full price than to have to rely on a thunderbolt or something.'

'How well we understand one another,' he said. 'It's been a pleasure to take your money. My last story is of an officer in the last war. How he got his commission was something of a mystery, but I think it was because he had registered at an early date with the Officers' Emergency Reserve and had a University degree. Somehow or other he held on to his commission and he eventually found himself with his battalion in North Africa. His CO loathed the sight of him, but, though he had tried several times to get rid of him, it had always just gone wrong and he stayed with the battalion. One day, after an exercise, the CO came upon him lying on the sand, having his lunch. He got up when he saw the CO. He knew enough for that, though he was comfortable on the sand and thought it rather a bore.

' "Have the men been fed?" said the CO.

' "I think they're just going to get theirs. There's been some hold-up or other. Shall I ask the Platoon Sergeant, sir?"

'The CO nearly burst. "Murray, you're a damned disgrace. How many times have I got to tell you that an officer doesn't feed before his men?"

' "I was rather hungry, sir."

' "You something, something, something," said the CO. "If we weren't going into action in a few days, I'd have you up before the brigadier. You're a lazy good-for-nothing something."

' "I'm very sorry, sir, but there didn't seem any point in waiting. If I'd shared my ration with the platoon, it wouldn't have gone anywhere."

' "Heaven give me patience," said the CO. "If ever I find you doing this again, I'll have you outed. D'you know what a 199E is?"

' "No idea, sir."

' "It's an adverse report. I ought to have made one on you months ago. Now, go and see where the men's rations are and don't you dare eat or drink till the last man's finished. That's an order."

' "Very good, sir."

'The CO can be excused his anger. Lieutenant Murray was undoubtedly lazy to a degree and worried far more about his own comforts than about his men. It seemed to him extremely stupid that he should have to starve when he'd a perfectly good haversack ration on him, just because the Colour Sergeant had made a bungle about his men's food. It never struck him that it was his responsibility to see that such a mistake did not occur.

'Well, eventually the battalion went into action. It was Alamein. The rifle companies went through the minefields and occupied a very sticky position in front of the enemy. There they were pretty well pinned to the ground and they dug themselves in as best they could. It was Murray's job to guide the medium machine-guns up to the battalion as soon as he was given the word, so that they could be dug in before dawn. Eventually, he received his orders over the wireless and off he started in a carrier, with the four trucks with the machine-guns behind. His carrier got temporarily stuck and, as there wasn't much time, he told the trucks to carry on, pointing out the general direction of what was supposed to be a gap in the minefield. Three trucks went up on mines and the machine-gun officer was badly wounded. Shortly afterwards the CO asked him on the wireless when the something something the MMG's were coming up.

' "Coming, sir," he had said.

' "Well – if you don't, we'll be wiped out. None of the Brens are working."

93

'For the first time Lieutenant Murray had to do some pretty rapid thinking. There was only one truck left. If that went up, the battalion was lost. There was obviously no gap in the minefield where they were. They must be off their course. He looked around to see if there were any sappers to help. There were none. Even if he'd dared, he couldn't ask the CO on the wireless: "Could you please tell me exactly where the gap is?" Even if he had, the answer would have been useless. It was night, and one piece of sand is singularly like another piece. Finally, Lieutenant Murray took a piece of chain which had broken off a blown-up flail tank and, by himself, lying at full length, made a gap in the minefield by the simple, but incredibly perilous, experiment of bringing down the chain and exploding any mines it hit. Why he wasn't killed is one of the many miracles that occur in a war. But he wasn't and, just before the dawn, he got the one and only MMG safely through to the battalion and dug in. The additional fire power saved the battalion. All the CO said to Lieutenant Murray was: "So you've only got one through. I might have known it. But I hope you've had your lunch?"

'Murray didn't actually hear what he said, as he had fainted from exhaustion. But a couple of shells landing nearby soon revived him. Eventually the battalion was relieved and came out of the line. No one was aware that it owed its safety to Murray and that officers have received the highest decoration for less than he had done. He had certainly found it a bit of an effort and very frightening, but he had no idea of the real quality of his feat. Shortly afterwards, while the battalion was behind the lines, the CO came on Murray having his lunch.

' "Have your men been fed?" demanded the CO.

'Murray smiled a trifle wearily. "Have you a 199E on you, sir? I'm afraid you'll need it."

'And, in due course, a 199E was filled in and Murray lost his commission. I think of him when I look at that picture over there. He was a man, wasn't he? Selfish and lazy – but the spark was in him just the same. In an hour or so this bar will be filled with greedy good-for-nothings, all trying to do each other down, all wanting to know the worst about the other. Oh for a war that makes them men! Sorry. I'm ranting rather.'

'That's all very well,' I said. 'I see your point. But you can't know that any of these stories are true. You couldn't have told the last story unless you'd been Murray himself, and he would never have told it.'

'That's fair enough. I've had to draw on my imagination for some of them. But the principle's there just the same, isn't it? You don't really need the examples once you've grasped that, do you? Today – he's a greedy scandalmonger – always sniffing around for a bit of dirt. But tomorrow – who knows? Anyway, one of these stories is true to my knowledge.'

'Which?'

'Well – Clarissa is upstairs now.'

'Then you must be – '

'That's right,' he said. 'I'm George.' And he smiled pleasantly at me.

Unkind Cut

In earlier days Charles might have been described, somewhat unfairly, as a ladies' man. Unfairly, because the word usually has and had a slightly unpleasant significance. All right perhaps on the stage when the character was played by a famous actor but otherwise suggesting a person whom most men and many women would cordially dislike. Charles was not at all such a person. He was generally popular and his relationship with women can perhaps be best and most fairly described by saying that he had confidence with them.

His confidence not only made him at ease when talking to them but swiftly put them at ease too. It is going too far to say that a prisoner would rather have five years from a judge who obviously meant to give it to him than to receive a lesser sentence from a judge who was 'not quite sure what to do with you'. But undoubtedly confidence breeds confidence and a judge who feels sure that he should give judgment for the plaintiff and makes it plain that he feels sure about it has more chance of persuading the unsuccessful defendant of the righteousness of the decision than the judge who says something like: 'This is a very difficult case and I do not hesitate to say that I have several times in the course of it had to change my ideas. Indeed, even now, I have considerable doubt as to the correctness of the view which I am about to express.

However, doing the best I can and recognising that another judge might have given a completely different decision, I have come to the conclusion on balance and, as I have said, not without hesitation, etc, etc, etc.'

In such a case the unsuccessful party is not at all consoled by his counsel informing him that he very nearly won. Losing (when you have nearly won) is far worse than never getting near a win at all.

And so it is, not only in the Courts but in daily life, and the man who displays an attractive confidence finds many friends. The easy persuasiveness of a great advocate is a most useful quality to possess. And undoubtedly Charles, though not a lawyer, had it.

He was much in demand at cocktail parties where, within a few seconds of introduction to a woman, he would be on apparently intimate terms with her. Most people like talking about themselves and cocktails are no discouragement. In consequence quite a number of men learn about the private affairs of complete strangers after, say, four or five Martinis. Applying that yardstick, one could fairly say that Charles was a one-Martini man. He seldom talked about himself, except to draw the person to whom he was talking, and there was almost nothing that some women would not tell him after quite a short acquaintanceship.

Charles would have been inhuman if he had not realised his gifts and he became supremely confident and sure of himself. So, if he was to have a fall, it was likely to be a heavy one.

One evening he took a few friends to dinner and they included an American and his charming and attractive American wife. Charles took them to the best restaurant he could think of. Unfortunately that is not very difficult in London. Over the drinks before dinner Charles' guests selected what they would have to eat and the Americans disregarded without hesitation the more exotic dishes and chose roast beef. Charles was not surprised, as he knew that English roast beef is one of the reasons why some Americans cross the Atlantic.

It was a very pleasant evening and Charles made full use of his charms. There appeared no doubt at all that the ladies in the party all fell for him, while the men found him a most agreeable host. He provided entertainment of every kind for such an occasion. When at last the party broke up, Charles drove the Americans back to their hotel. When they got there he helped them out of the car, shook hands with the husband and kissed the wife. They were going back to America the next day and very possibly they would never meet again, and certainly not for a long time. No husband could have objected to Charles' familiarity. The wife, so far from objecting, responded with interest and, in spite of his years of confidence, Charles could not help feeling pleased that he had made an impression in so short a time. He even began to wish that the husband would take a stroll, so that he could repeat the experience. But this was impossible. So he contented himself with maintaining the clinch as long as was decent before they separated. Then the attractive young woman started to say something and Charles began to think of the strongest reply he could make without either annoying the husband or too grossly exaggerating. The girl was obviously going to say something like: 'You're rather sweet,' or something he could treasure with the memory of the embrace. He kept quite a small store of such memories and pleasantly recalled them to himself when he had nothing better to do. And then she spoke. It took Charles several days to recover. 'That was the most lovely roast beef I've ever eaten,' she said.

Near Miss

Some people say that politics is a dirty game and that politicians are not to be trusted, but, even so, most of them would have accepted Giles Kenwood, MP as a man of integrity. And he was. In 1961 he had reached a very important stage in his career, and there was a strong chance that he would receive a ministerial appointment. In March of that year he had started a road safety campaign which for the first time had attracted the notice of the public. His argument for the campaign had been a simple one. If only people took a little more care the accident rate would be halved. The problem was to prove this to the public. Eventually, by the force of his speeches in Parliament and at public meetings, his letters to the Press and his strong arguments at interviews with the heads of various organisations concerned with road safety, he persuaded the Government to organise a national No-Accident Day when it was to be a point of honour among the population as a whole not to be involved in an accident. If the accident rate dropped on that day he would have given the public the proof which was required. It would not necessarily mean the immediate permanent reduction of the accident rate but it would mean that the first positive step in that direction had been taken. Each member of the public would have been given definite proof that a little extra care on his or her part could save seven or eight lives a day.

It had not been easy to move the Government but in the end he had persuaded them to try the idea and, preceded by a concentrated campaign in the Press, on radio and television, in the churches and schools, by posters in the streets and every known method of advertising, the great day arrived. Kenwood had himself taken a great part in the campaign, and the probability was that, if it succeeded, he would become the next Minister of Transport.

The weather was kindly on the great day and it was with some relief that Kenwood and his wife heard that throughout the country visibility was good and the roads were dry. He took his wife out in the car in the morning to do some shopping. He felt elated. It was true that, if the accident rate did not drop, he would have been proved wrong, but at least his idea would have been tried. Penal legislation against motorists would have no effect. Motorists were by no means the only people to blame. Moreover, even in cases where they were, there were not enough police to catch them and juries were very slow to convict them. But here was something which involved no penalty for anyone. Just a little extra care, that was all that was asked. Surely it would work. It had failed in the United States, but that was a huge country divided into States which were in many respects independent and where it was very hard, if not impossible, to make an impact on every individual in a matter of this kind. But whether or not it failed here, it was taking place. Something at any rate was being done.

He drove carefully, as he always did. He certainly was not going to have an accident that day. He came to some crossroads, looked right and left, saw nothing and drove across them. As he arrived safely in the road opposite, his wife gave a little scream.

'What's the matter?' he asked.

'Didn't you see that cyclist?'

'What cyclist?'

'What cyclist! The one coming along the road. I thought he was bound to hit you. He would have, if he hadn't braked for all he was worth and followed you round.'

Kenwood looked in his mirror and saw a cyclist following him. He was on a bright blue, semi-racing bicycle.

'I never saw any cyclist,' he said. 'But he was coming round here anyway.'

'He wasn't, I assure you,' said his wife. 'He was going hard at right angles to you. It's a miracle there wasn't an accident.'

Kenwood looked again in his mirror and saw the cyclist turn round and disappear in the direction in which his wife said he had been going.

'Good God!' he said. 'You were right. I never saw the man.'

'I was sure you had or I'd have said something,' said his wife.

'Good God!' Kenwood repeated.

'D'you think we should go back and speak to him?'

'Well, he's gone now, and there wasn't an accident.'

'He may have taken your number.'

'We could never find him. We can't go up to every cyclist and say: "Did I nearly knock you down?" '

'Well, let's hope he hasn't taken your number.'

'Don't keep on saying that,' he said sharply. He never spoke to his wife like that. 'I'm sorry, darling,' he added. 'I was just a bit worried for a moment. Thank Heaven he wasn't hurt. But I'd look pretty silly charged with careless driving.'

'But you're never careless.'

'I must have been. I think I see how it happened. I must have been unsighted by you and the parcels and the door pillar combined. A cycle coming head-on is a pretty small object and I must have missed seeing him that way.'

'Well, there you are,' said his wife, 'if he has got your number, that's your defence.'

'It isn't a defence,' said Kenwood. 'If you can't see for certain that the road is clear, you've no business to cross. I ought to have realised the amount of obstruction there was to my view and that a cyclist might be hidden behind it.'

'I expect he was too shaken to get your number. We were probably fifty yards away before his heart started to beat again.'

'Well, if he has got it, I shall look a pretty good fool. On today of all days, too. Think what some of the chaps who've opposed me could make of it.'

'If today's a success, it won't matter.'

'Won't it, though! They'll take it out of me more than ever – out of pique, if you like. The leader of the campaign pleading guilty to careless driving! Whether it's a success or not, I can't see myself at the Ministry of Transport just yet with that against me.'

'But why plead guilty?'

'Because I was guilty. It'd be even worse to try to fight it.'

'Well, cheer up. I don't suppose he could get the number.'

She changed the subject, but her husband was still brooding on the matter. Suppose the man had taken his number, he'd rush to the nearest police station.

'I've just nearly been killed by a car,' he'd say, 'but I've got the number fortunately. The fellow didn't stop, and tore away.'

He hadn't torn away, but anyone who had nearly been involved in such an accident would certainly think he had. And say so. The Sergeant would take the number and put an enquiry through the Council where his car was registered. Then they'd have to send a policeman to see him.

'Forgive my troubling you, sir,' the policeman would say, 'but I'm making enquiries about an incident at the crossroads where Bignal Road crosses Hampshire Street. A cyclist has stated ...' and so on and so on, until finally he'd ask: 'The car appears to be registered in your name, sir. Can you tell me who was driving it at the time?'

Well, he'd have to admit that he was. It would be unthinkable to hedge, or refuse to answer. No doubt the cyclist would be unable to identify him, but he would probably say a man was driving. He couldn't pretend it was some other man or that he didn't know what the policeman was talking about. He'd have to come clean and make the best excuse he could. He'd point out, if necessary, how easy it is to become unsighted by a near object. Sometimes even a lamp-post can unsight you from an object as big as a car. But then, of course, they'd say he shouldn't have driven across. And, of course, he shouldn't. Perhaps they wouldn't prosecute. But how could they do otherwise? It might look bad if anyone heard about it. 'Can the Attorney-General tell the House why no proceedings were taken against the honourable member for Underwood?' It was an open and shut case, once he admitted that he was there driving the car. And he'd have to. And the headlines! Oh, God!

'Which would you prefer to see, darling?' said his wife. She had been talking about plays. They were going to celebrate their wedding anniversary by going to the theatre. He hadn't heard a word. Somehow or other he took his mind off the cyclist and discussed the celebration, but it was not easy. Once anxiety gets into the mind it tends to increase to alarming proportions. When he managed to discuss the choice of plays it helped him for a few minutes.

A moment later he was back again with the policeman on his doorstep. But would he come? Had the man taken his number? When would he know? And then a horrible thought came to him. He would have to wait fourteen days before he knew. He was aware that a man cannot be charged with careless driving unless he's warned at the time of the offence or unless he receives a summons or a warning letter within fourteen days of the incident. Fourteen days! How could he endure fourteen days of what he'd suffered in the last minutes? Every knock at the door – would it be a policeman? Every time he came home – had a policeman called in his absence?

This led him to another line of thought. What was his wife to say if a policeman did call when he was out? Well, he supposed, she must do the same as he would. Tell the whole truth. Any thought of prevarication by a man in his position, or by his wife, would be terribly bad. At least he would have that in his favour, that he hadn't tried to evade the issue. But hadn't he? He hadn't tried to find the cyclist and he hadn't reported the incident to a police station. Should he do so? Was it his duty? There hadn't been an accident, so there was no legal duty to report what had happened. But he couldn't rely very much on his frankness to a policeman if he was only frank when he was found out.

But perhaps the man hadn't taken his number. It's very difficult to get the number of a receding car unless you start to do so when it is very close. His wife may have been right. The man may have been so shaken that he didn't start to take it until too late. He was rather ashamed of the thought, particularly because he couldn't help hoping that that had happened. Fourteen days of this, he thought. Can I stand it? It'll be torture. But it's ridiculous, he told himself. You haven't broken into a bank, or murdered someone. Just a slight mistake. No one hurt. And it could happen to anyone. But someone was nearly hurt. Might have been killed. That's exactly how people were killed. Because someone didn't take quite enough care. Those were his own words on television. "Because someone didn't take quite enough care." No, he was the one person to whom this must not happen. He would be the world's laughing stock. "Just that little bit of extra care," he remembered saying. "It won't cost you anything in money. Only a second or two in time. And thousands of lives may be saved if you'll give it. I appeal to you all …" He turned off the broadcast in his mind. It would be too dreadful. He, of all people, had not taken just that little bit of extra care which he had implored everyone else to take. And on this day of all days.

He could visualise the headlines: 'Road Safety MP Pleads Guilty to Careless Driving.' He could visualise the report: 'Mr Abercrombie, on behalf of Mr Kenwood, said that his client much regretted …' or should he just write a letter?

'Or would you prefer the show at the Criterion?'

It was his wife speaking again. He managed to reply coherently. He felt ashamed of his fears and for once did not wish to share them with his wife. He knew it was pure cowardice.

Somehow or other he got through the day. Fortunately he was very much occupied, though, each time he had a moment to himself, his mind returned to the subject. But it was only after the House rose and he was on his way home that another thought occurred to him. Supposing the cyclist had only got part of his number, say all but one letter, it might be impossible to trace him within fourteen days. Surely the law didn't let a hit-and-run driver get away with it if he couldn't be traced for fourteen days? He wasn't a hit-and-run driver, but the principle was exactly the same. If fourteen days went by before it was possible to trace a man who didn't stop, could no proceedings take place, however quickly the police had worked? He would have to find out the next day but, if his belief were correct, even at the end of fourteen days he would not be safe.

He reached home, chatted to his wife about the proceedings in the House and then went to bed. His wife was soon asleep but, as he had feared, sleep for him was impossible. There were so many questions to be answered. Would the man have been likely to go to the police? No doubt he was shaken, but that would soon wear off. He hadn't been hurt. Why should he bother? But perhaps he was one of those determined people who pursue things to the end. He had been wronged, the wrongdoer did not stop; he had his number and would see that he was brought to justice. If he was that sort of person, how long would it take? Presumably the police could get the information on the telephone and, if so, they'd send down to his house pretty quickly. The next day, probably. So, if they didn't come the next day or the day after, perhaps he'd be all right. But the police were busy people and there was a lot of serious crime. A mere case of careless driving, when there was no accident, might be put aside for a few days. But they'd surely come within the first week. They knew of the fourteen-day rule. That meant seven nights like this one. He couldn't stand it. He'd get some sleeping tablets and take them for a week.

But suppose the man had nearly got the number but wasn't quite sure. It was either IKP, JKP or YKP and the figures were 984. They'd have to investigate all three numbers and he might come last. That would take time. Or perhaps he wasn't sure of one of the figures either. How many permutations would that make? It would vastly increase the number of possibilities. Could take well over the fortnight then. Then, of course, he might have got all the letters and digits except one. That could mean twenty-five possibilities. But, if he wasn't sure of one of the letters *and* one of the figures, it would mean hundreds. He couldn't take sleeping tablets for months. But he couldn't endure this strain either.

Then he would pull himself together for a moment. What am I worrying about? Probably the man hasn't got the number or isn't doing anything about it. But at the worst it was just a mistake – one mistake in twenty years of driving. He tried to sleep for a little. But his mind wasn't having that. One mistake, it said, but a man might have been killed by it. And so he went through the night, occasionally sleeping and dreaming but mostly turning over and over and worrying.

'Anything the matter, darling?' asked his wife in the morning, when she saw how tired he looked. 'Not still worrying about that cyclist?'

He spoke as casually as he could:

'Not really. But it oughtn't to have happened. If a policeman does happen to call ...'

'A policeman! You poor darling. You have been worrying. No policeman is going to call. You'll see. Now what time will they get the figures for yesterday?'

He'd almost forgotten what yesterday was.

'Not till late afternoon, I'm told. The late editions of the evening papers should have it in.'

And they did. It had been a resounding success. Only about half the number of accidents. Less than half the average number of people killed – a third of the number injured. He was congratulated on all sides and for a short time was able to forget his anxiety. But on the way home it started again. His wife couldn't have got hold of him during the day to tell him if a policeman had called. He'd just have to wait till he got home. He'd know at once then. It would be the first thing she'd say if anything had happened.

He arrived. His wife was upstairs.

'Hello, darling,' she called down. 'Well done.' She had heard the news of the success on No-Accident day.

Thank God! he said to himself. Nothing can have happened.

She came downstairs and kissed him.

'I got a shock this morning,' she said a few minutes later. 'A policeman called.'

He went white. Then it had happened. Oh, God!

She was not looking at him as she spoke, and did not realise the effect on him of what she said.

'It was only about my bicycle. I'd left it in Hammer Street again.'

The relief was great but the horror was still there.

'I think I'd like a drink,' he said.

'Of course. Sherry?'

'No – whisky – a large one, please.'

'Whisky? But you never touch it.'

'Please, darling,' he said, 'I would like one.' During that day he had found out that his belief about the fourteen days not being an absolutely rigid rule was right. It didn't apply if the owner of the car could not reasonably have been traced within that time. So how long had he got to wait? Weeks? Months? And then another unpleasant

108

thought had occurred to him. If they didn't call until after the fourteen days, it was because they had got to trace a lot of numbers. That meant that, if the police did call, he had only to say that he hadn't been anywhere near the place of the incident on the occasion in question and he would be safe. The cyclist would never be able to identify him. His car was dark in colour. Well, so were lots of cars. If he and his wife said they weren't there, nothing could happen. The policeman would apologise for troubling him and try the next number. He would be completely safe and no one but himself and his wife would ever know the truth. It was a horrible thought. If he lasted the fourteen days he'd be safe ever after, if he were prepared to lie. He had a moment or two's struggle with the situation. But it did not take him long to make up his mind. He would have to tell the truth, whatever the consequences. He could not go through life knowing that he had lied and, almost as bad, with his wife knowing that he had done so too. She was far less scrupulous than he was and he had no doubt that she would cheerfully lie to save him, if he asked her, and worry not at all about it. But he'd too often criticised such an attitude and he couldn't let her see him adopt it himself.

He took sleeping tablets that night and slept better. The next day he was told confidentially that in about three months' time the Minister of Transport was going to retire and he would be offered the job. Things were looking up. He had been cheered when he entered the House and no policeman had yet called. He felt he must have some excuse to telephone his wife during the day, just to be sure that nothing had happened.

'Did I by any chance leave a letter on the dining-room table?'

'A letter? I didn't see one. I'll look.'

It was all right. If a policeman had called she'd have told him at once.

After the first week he felt distinctly better. Surely the police would have called by now if the man had got his number. They might still be tracing numbers but, if they did eventually come to him, it would at least be in his favour that he told the police at once when he could have got out of it by a lie. He stopped taking sleeping tablets. He still telephoned his wife unnecessarily during the day, just to be sure, but now he was becoming more confident that he would not be greeted with bad news.

At last the fourteen days were over and he felt fairly safe. And, as the weeks went on, although he did not forget the incident, it ceased to worry him. And the thought that he would soon be a Minister of the Crown was a very pleasant one. He became a normal person again.

And then one day, when he came back from the House, tired but happy, his wife said as soon as he arrived: 'Giles, while I was out two men called and said they wanted to see you.'

'Two men?'

He was still not worried. If it had happened ten weeks before, he'd have gone white, as he did when his wife told him about the policeman calling about her bicycle.

'Yes, Mrs Main said they were from Scotland Yard.'

'Scotland Yard!'

He did go white.

'What did they want?'

'They didn't say, but they're coming first thing in the morning. I wonder what it is, darling. You don't think it could still be about that cyclist?'

'I don't know. I don't think so. That's surely not a Scotland Yard matter. They'd have sent a local policeman to see us.'

Although he said that to his wife, he said to himself that perhaps, when numbers were difficult to trace, it was handed over to Scotland Yard. Now he'd have to wait till the morning to know. Probably it was about a burglary somewhere, or something. Or perhaps it was political and they were from the Special Branch. And yet all the time he felt it must be about the cyclist. He could see the headlines again: 'Minister of Transport Pleads Guilty to Careless Driving.' But it wouldn't be that. If he were going to be prosecuted, he couldn't accept the job. He took two sleeping tablets and slept so soundly that he was actually woken up by the knock at the door.

His wife opened it and showed the two men into the sitting room. Then she went back to the bedroom.

'It's them,' she said.

Well, at least now I'll know. No more waiting and worrying. But wouldn't there be? Waiting for the case to come on and wondering what would be made of it. But they must be from the Special Branch. Please, they must be, he said to himself, after all this time.

He put on his dressing-gown and went to the men.

'Good morning, sir.'

'Good morning. What can I do for you?'

'I'm Detective-Inspector Martin, sir, and this is Sergeant Doyle, from Scotland Yard.'

'Yes?'

'I'm making enquiries about an incident which is said to have taken place at the crossroads Bignal Road and Hampshire Street, on the 23rd of February last.'

God! So it had caught up with him after all. There can't have been two incidents on that day at that place about which they'd come to speak to him.

'Yes?' he said.

'A cyclist has stated that about 11.30 a.m. on that day he very nearly collided with a dark car which came across his path and didn't stop. I don't suppose it was you by any chance, sir? Yours is one of the possible numbers.'

This was it. After all these weeks of freedom. Prospective Minister of Transport!

'Yes, Inspector, it was. I never saw the man. My wife and her parcels must have obscured the view.'

'Well, I'm damned,' said the inspector. 'Excuse me, sir, I apologise. But when you've made over a hundred calls, you get to the stage when you never expect to find the man. As a matter of fact, we didn't believe there was one. But you can't take chances with murder.'

Kenwood's head swam. He went white, and felt for a chair to steady himself.

'Are you all right, sir?' asked the inspector.

'But he wasn't hurt. I never touched him,' said Kenwood. 'I know I didn't. My wife can confirm it. She'll tell you. She saw the man all the time and thought I had too, or she'd have warned me. And afterwards we saw him cycling behind me. He was on a bright blue bicycle. Then he turned round and disappeared.'

'Bright blue, did you say, sir?' said the inspector. 'Well I'm ... d'you mind if we sit down, sir? This has been a bit of a shock to us.'

'Please do. But the man wasn't hurt, I assure you. It must have been another car which ran over him. But I didn't read anything about it in the papers. I'll call my wife.'

He went straight out and brought her in.

'These are police officers who've called about the cyclist. They say he's dead – been murdered.'

'Oh no, sir, forgive me. I didn't say that. I said you can't take chances with a case of murder, and capital murder at that. The man who nearly collided with you is suspected of a murder in Birmingham. He's sworn all along that he was in London at the time, but he's got no one to back him up. Then he told us he'd nearly had an accident with a car which went across his path and didn't stop. He'd got its number but, after he'd cooled down, decided to do nothing about it. He'd written the number down on a book of matches which he'd still got, but it was so damaged when we interviewed him that we couldn't make out all the letters and figures. So we've been going through all the possible numbers just to see if there was any truth in it. A tedious process, sir. Lucky for him it was you, sir. Might have been one of those hit-and-run drivers who'd have been frightened to admit it.'

'And lucky you didn't see him,' said the sergeant.

'Lucky? Why?'

'Where would his alibi have been, sir, if you had?'

The Good Turn

It started at the Old Boys' dinner.

'Don't tell me,' said the prosperous-looking man. 'I know. It's Flintlock.'

'It's Summers, as a matter of fact.'

'Of course. You haven't changed really. I'd have known you anywhere. What about me? Have I changed?'

'Well,' said Summers, 'I've seen your picture in the papers so often that it's difficult to say. I couldn't help recognising you. You *have* done well.'

'You've followed my career with interest, have you, what!'

'Well, it's nice to see people one admired at school getting on afterwards.'

'I don't know what there was to admire about me at school. I never got my first eleven colours and you did. And you were always above me in form.'

'No, that was Flintlock. I was always just below.'

'Were you really now? I'd forgotten. And how have things been going?'

'Oh – not too bad.'

That was about an accurate description of Summers' position in the world. Not too bad. But not too good either. He managed, but that was all. Very different from that of the man he was talking to. Alan Crombie had become a really important person in the city. His photograph had indeed appeared in the newspapers fairly often. Sometimes in *The Times* at directors' meetings of important companies. Sometimes in the cheaper newspapers when there were rumours of a takeover bid.

Summers had idolised Crombie at school. Not for any particular reason. It happens like that. Whatever Crombie said Summers agreed with. Crombie only had to say 'Let's – ' and, whatever it was, Summers would say 'Yes'. This was useful to Crombie, for an immediate 'Yes' from one boy was a definite help towards obtaining general approval.

They never met after they left school until this particular Old Boys' dinner. Summers had attended many such gatherings, often with difficulty finding the price of the ticket. Crombie had had no time for such meetings. But now they had asked him to be President, and that was different. It was not only that he was complimented by it, but it was in its way quite useful. When your old school, which had never taken the slightest notice of you since you left, asks you to become President of the Old Boys' Association, you really have arrived.

'Tell me, my dear chap,' said Crombie, 'what do you do?'

It was not just a polite question. His own success made him take a sentimental interest in less successful old boys, and there was something a little pathetic about Summers. Without being told, he could see that he either had a small job with too little salary and no prospects or a small business which just managed to keep on the right side of insolvency.

'Nothing very thrilling,' said Summers. 'I've a small manufacturing business. Plastics, you know.'

'Ah, plastics. There's a lot to be done with them yet. We can wear them, build with them and eat them so far. You wait till we can split the atom in them. Public company?'

'Oh – no – very private and very small. We're not doing too badly, but it's the tax business that gets me down. To begin with, I can't understand it. That wouldn't matter so much, but I can't afford it.'

'Who's your accountant?' Crombie suddenly began to think how he might do his old schoolfellow a good turn.

'Just a small man. Like me – really.'

'Nonsense! What's his name?'

'Oh – you wouldn't know him. He's not really qualified, as a matter of fact.'

'Not qualified!' There was almost alarm in Crombie's voice. His business and private affairs were almost entirely done at the dictation of accountants. That was the only way in which a rich man could live like a rich man. But they were highly qualified accountants. Three Scottish and three English chartered accountants were the partners in the firm. One of them was President of the English Institute and another had passed the Chair. The idea of anyone going to an unqualified man was horrible. He could picture a little man, far more down-at-heel than Summers, living in a small furnished room and surrounded by papers, many of them in the wrong bundles. Dirty pipes lying all round the room and tobacco stains on some of the papers. Trailing to the ground from a broken-down armchair would be the uncompleted profit and loss account of the small grocery business round the corner and, no doubt, it contained several wrong computations. On some dusty shelves round the walls some even dustier files, few of them containing what the torn label on the outside stated. He could see the old man – he decided that he was old and that his name was Higginbottom – he could see him looking hopelessly through file after file to find a document which perhaps he had never received or had let fall into the waste-paper basket. Crombie had a vivid imagination and part of his success had been due to the fact that he was so often right.

'What's his name?' he asked.

'It's Roberts, as a matter of fact,' said Summers apologetically. It seemed almost an insult to his mighty friend to have to admit that his accountant was unqualified and that his name was just Roberts – not even Roberts and Co or Roberts and Roberts – but just plain Roberts.

Crombie was a little disappointed that it was not Higginbottom, but that was perhaps too much to expect.

'Tell me about him,' he went on. 'What are his offices like?'

'He hasn't exactly got an office,' said Summers. 'He does his work at home.'

'Have you been there?'

'Yes – once.'

'What was it like?'

'Oh – nothing very much, you know. It was just a room.'

'Dirty pipes lying around and in a pretty good mess?'

'Why – yes. How on earth did you know?'

'Oh – one learns these things, you know. It's my job to understand people. That's half the battle. Now it's jolly lucky we met tonight. I can do you a good turn.'

'That's very decent of you, Crombie.'

'Not at all, old man, not at all. Only too pleased. Now, let me tell you something. This is the era of accountants. There are no good businesses and no bad businesses. There are just good accountants and bad accountants. It's as simple as that.'

'Is that really so? I knew they'd become more important but I didn't know it was to that extent.'

'Believe me, old boy, I know what I'm talking about. They run the country. Some people don't realise it. But that's how it is. Now look, I've got a house in the country, a flat in town, a Rolls Royce and two smaller cars, I fly wherever I go luxury class, I can give my wife the clothes she wants – and that's saying something I can tell you – and I pay 17/9 in the £ on most of my income. Sounds impossible, doesn't it? Well, it would be, if I didn't have the best accountants in the world. I'm not saying there aren't other good firms of accountants. Of course there are. Plenty of them. But mine are the tops. Now, if you'd been going to Price Waterhouse or someone like that, I shouldn't have said a word. And it wouldn't have been necessary. Your business would have been fine. But little Mr Roberts in the Old Kent Road – '

'It's the New Kent Road, as a matter of fact.'

'Good gracious – is it really? Well – as long as you have your little Mr Roberts in the New Kent Road you'll never get on – never. Now I'll tell you what I'll do. I don't suppose Hope, Chevely – those are my people – would want to take over a small one-man business in the ordinary way, but I'll drop a note to Chevely and he'll take you on. No doubt about it.'

'It's awfully kind of you, Crombie.'

'Not in the least, old boy. Only too pleased. And you'll see the difference in no time. They'll charge you a bit more, of course, but it'll be worth it. You take my word for it. What does Mr Higginbottom – I mean Roberts – charge you?'

'Well, you're quite right – he doesn't charge very much – ten or twenty guineas a year, I suppose.'

'Ten or twenty guineas! When you pay your accountants a *hundred* and ten or twenty guineas you'll know things are improving. No – don't worry,' he added hastily, as he saw an anxious look on Summers' face, 'I'll tell Chevely he's only to make a nominal charge until you're on your feet.'

'No – really – that'd be an imposition.'

'Imposition – my foot! D'you know what we pay them? Well – I don't know myself, but it's something fantastic. But is it worth it? You'll see. D'you know, they've saved us hundreds of thousands of pounds in tax. They're real experts. Some of the cases which go to the House of Lords are directly due to Chevely himself – and he's only once been wrong. And then it was only by a majority of three to two in the House of Lords. The Court of Appeal and the judge of first instance said he was right. Funny thing the law. Six judges said Chevely was right and only three said he was wrong. But the word of the three had it. Still it's not a bad record.'

'Remarkable,' said Summers. 'But I'd hardly like to trouble them with my little affairs.'

'Don't be so bashful. Your little affairs may be big affairs one day. You may split the plastic atom. Then you'll be paying Hope, Chevely five figures a year. But mark my words. You can split as many atoms as you like, but you'll do no good without proper accountants. I expect they'll find your affairs in the most hopeless disorder. You can't expect anything else from the Mr Robertses of this world.'

And a week later Crombie's prophecy turned out, as usual, to be true. One of Messrs Hope, Chevely's clerks turned over Summers' papers with a pained expression, rather like that of a Rolls Royce salesman when asked if his firm could supply a second-hand car for not more than about five hundred pounds.

'I'm afraid,' he said to Mr Summers, 'that we shall have to do a lot of work on these. Please don't think I'm criticising your former accountant – I shouldn't dream of doing so-but some of his working papers are quite meaningless and there are some definite mistakes in arithmetic, I'm afraid. Wrong casting and so on.'

'I'm very sorry,' said Summers.

'Oh, that's quite all right, Mr Summers,' said the clerk. 'It's not your responsibility. But it does mean that this will take rather longer than I'd hoped. However, we'll have it all right for you in the end.'

And in the end they did. They cleared up all Mr Roberts' mistakes, they interviewed the tax inspector several times, they eventually agreed everything with him and finally handed Summers a beautifully drawn up bundle of accounts with all the trimmings to be expected from a firm of the standing of Hope, Chevely and Co.

Not long afterwards Crombie and Summers met again. 'My dear Flintlock – no, of course, it's Summers – how are you?'

'Not too bad, thank you. It was kind of you to send me to your accountants.'

'Oh – of course – you were worried about tax matters. I remember. Well, I bet it's made a difference to you. I told you they were the people. Did they fix things with your tax inspector? I don't suppose your little Mr Higginbottom ever saw him.'

'Well – that's what I'd rather like to ask you about, if you can spare a moment. As a matter of fact this isn't a chance meeting. I thought you'd be here and came on purpose. I hope you don't mind.'

It is usually pleasant to have done someone a good turn, and, if anyone dislikes being reminded of it, it is the beneficiary, not the benefactor.

'Mind, old boy? Of course not. We must meet more often. What can I do for you?'

'Well, it's like this. You were quite right. Mr Roberts *had* made a pretty good mess of things and Hope, Chevely have straightened it all out.'

'Fine, fine. Well, what's the question?'

'Well – it's just this – ' Summers hesitated.

'Come on, old boy – out with it. Were their fees a bit steep? I'm sure I asked Chevely – '

Summers interrupted. 'Oh – no – they were most reasonable, indeed they only made a nominal charge. It was most kind of you to speak to them about it.'

'Then what is it, old boy?'

'Well, it's a little embarrassing but – to come to the point – my Mr Roberts hadn't been to see the tax people but they *had* agreed his accounts. Now Hope, Chevely have found out that I've underpaid about fifteen hundred pounds over the last five years. I suppose – you couldn't by any chance – '

The Nightmare

Basil Merridew and Nicholas Drewe liked high living but disliked real work. Each of them had an attractive wife. Basil's wife Elizabeth was superlatively so. The two couples lived on their wits, which were quite considerable. Their most satisfactory exploit from their point of view was to persuade the members of a country community to slander Basil. Posing as uncle and nephew, Basil and Nicholas had taken a small house in the country, near Poppleton. Basil behaved monstrously and was most unpopular. Nicholas was liked by all. When feelings against Basil had been sufficiently inflamed they put their plan into action.

Basil was apparently pursued by creditors and likely to have the bailiffs in at any moment. Having grossly insulted and humiliated a woman, who up to that time had been the only person to have a good word for him, he announced to her that he had had an unfortunate burglary and lost a valuable stamp collection. She, in fury at her humiliation, had rushed off to a cocktail party, where she announced the news of the burglary. Everyone said it was a fake to get the insurance money, and the popular Nicholas, who was there, heard it all.

Unfortunately for the slanderers, Basil was not insured and they all had to withdraw their allegations and pay heavy damages. Basil and Nicholas then left the neighbourhood.

But the money which they obtained did not last for ever and the time came when some other method had to be devised of getting the good things out of life without paying for them. The awful idea of having to work for a living began to appear horribly near to them. One day Basil was sitting in an armchair, trying unsuccessfully to devise a new plan to avoid the necessity for putting that grim idea into painful practice, when gradually he fell into a sleep. And he dreamed. And this was the dream.

'Wake up, wake up,' he heard Nicholas say.

'What is it?' he answered sleepily.

'You've an interview with the Bedside Manor Property Company Ltd. Come on. Out of it. You're due there in half an hour.'

Twenty minutes later, Basil was on his way to the Company's offices. He had apparently applied for the job of rent collector and had been short-listed.

'So you're Mr Basil Merridew,' said the secretary of the Company. 'I shouldn't have thought so from your handwriting.'

'Indeed?' said Basil.

'Indeed,' replied the secretary. 'Your handwriting is neat and tidy.'

'I'm afraid my wife writes my letters for me.'

'Well, she won't be able to do this job for you. Too tough for a woman.'

'May I have full details of the position?'

'That is what you are here for. The Company has 700 tenants in your area. You are to collect the rents from each once a week. The salary is £7 per week and one-half per cent of the rent collected. The average weekly rent in your area is 30/-. So, if they all paid, you'd bring back about £1000 each week. In that case, you'd get just over £5 above your salary. Got it?'

'I haven't checked your figures.'

'I shouldn't bother. You'll have plenty to do checking figures later.'

'Why is that?'

'Because of the arrears. I said the job was too tough for a woman. It's too tough for some men. Many of our tenants don't like paying rent. They get into arrear. Then we sue them in the County Court. The kindly County Court judge says something like this: "What are the arrears?"

'Our solicitor replies: "£37. 8s. 41/2 d., your Honour."

' "Dear, dear," says the judge, "that's a great deal. How has that happened?" and he turns to the tenant's wife, who is holding the latest of her babies. The tenant isn't present. The drill is that either he's at work or in hospital or, any way, it's more convenient to send the wife.

' "Oh, your Worship," says the tenant's wife, "my husband's been out of work owing to illness, but he's just started again."

' "I see," says the judge, "but you'll understand I mustn't be generous with someone else's money. The current rent is £1, 3s. 9d. How much can you pay off the arrears each week?"

' "I thought 25/- altogether, your Worship. We've eight children."

' "Dear, dear," says the judge, "that's not your landlord's fault. What do you say, Mr Bump?"

'Bump is our solicitor. He isn't much good but he's the nephew of our managing director and we have to use him.

' "Oh, well, your Honour," he says, with a wry smile, "these arrears have been piling up, and I would most respectfully suggest to your Honour that the defendant should pay a little more."

' "Have you eight children, Mr Bump?"

'Well, you can see how it's going to end. Bump always does what the judge tells him. If he doesn't do it when the judge asks him with a pleasant smile, he does it when the judge – in judicial language, of course – calls him all the names under the sun, adding at the end that he realises he mustn't be generous with the plaintiff's money.

'Now, when you meet that little lady – the tenant's wife – who was so sweet and (if necessary) tearful in the witness box, you'll find she isn't quite so sweet to you. And, if anyone cries after the interview, it'll probably be you. If you meet her husband, you'll probably apologise for troubling him about the rent, but you won't stay too long apologising – not if you're like the man you'll be replacing. He's on the sick list. Got a broken jaw. That tenant's inside. The beak gave him three months. But his wife's still there. Now, of course, she's got a better excuse than ever for not paying the rent. No use taking her to Court.

' "Dear, dear," the judge would say. "What are we to do, Mr Bump?"

'Bump would give his sickly grin and say, "Of course, my clients don't want to be hard on the defendant." It's quite untrue. His clients want to be very hard on the defendant, but nobody will let them, not even their own solicitor.

' "Thank you, Mr Bump," the judge would say, "it's most generous of your clients. We'll adjourn the case for six months, shall we? That'll give him time to get back to work when he comes out. I hope you'll manage all right, madam," he would add to the lady. "Most distressing for you."

'He doesn't mention the broken jaw. Right. Here's your bag. Don't let anyone snatch it from you. That's another thing. The bright boys in the neighbourhood will soon know who you are and one day one of them may ask you for a light while another one relieves you of the miserable amount you've collected. A third may bash you on the head. Good morning. Don't forget your rent roll.'

The Bedside Manor Property Company Ltd had a varied assortment of tenements. Some were single houses with no steps to climb. If no one was in, you could simply go to the next. Others had anything up to six floors. Before he took the job, Basil had never even thought of rent collectors. He sent the rent for his flat quarterly by cheque and had never considered how the rents of weekly tenants were dealt with. He soon learned.

Up the stairs of a five-storey building he would go. Perhaps they happened to be good tenants up there – regular with their rent and pleasant about paying it. Two of them in, three of them out. He comes back again. One of the three in. The other two out. And so on. He was dead tired before half the day was gone.

During the short period in which he had the job, Basil learned the ways of nearly every kind of weekly tenant, the good, the bad, the tearful, the cheerful, the clean, the dirty, the playful, the surly, those who spent the rent on drink, those who spent it on horses and dogs, and those who divided it fairly equally between the three, with an occasional portion for the landlord; this was usually when racing had been cancelled owing to bad weather. He never knew that his feet and legs could ache so much.

On one occasion when he had climbed up six flights of stairs for the third time in one day, he knocked at a door. Nothing happened. He knocked again. Suddenly, the door started to open slowly, but he saw nothing at first. Then he looked down and saw a very small boy of about four.

'Hullo, rascal,' said Basil. He was fond of children and still trying to be cheerful.

The child just looked at him.

'Well, rascal, where's your mother?'

'In the boozer, rascal,' piped a small voice.

'D'you know when she'll be back?'

The small thing shook its head.

'In the boozer,' it repeated.

Down the stairs went Basil and, on the ground floor, whom should he meet but the tenant's wife?

'Well, well,' he said, 'this is a bit of luck.'

'Better come up, dearie,' said the lady, a little sleepily.

Basil went up with her and twice prevented her from falling down the stairs. When they'd reached the top, the lady said: 'It's a shame dragging you all the way up, dearie.'

'That's all right,' said Basil, getting out his book. 'That's what I'm paid for.'

'Yes, dearie,' said the lady, 'but if only you'd come yesterday I'd have had the rent. But I met that Mrs Parker at the Rose & Crown and what with one thing and another and her old man having been took bad again, we got talking, and honest, dearie, I'd meant to keep the rent, but you know how it is. I've only fourpence ha'penny left. My old man won't half kick up a row when he gets back. It's his dogs' night. Still, better be lucky than rich, I say. I'll have it for you next week, honest I will, and a bit off the old. It is a shame you coming up all this way for nothing. Now, Charlie, you get in at once or I'll pay you.'

Sadly Basil went down the stairs for the fourth time that day. A thin-lipped woman opened the door to him at the next house.

'Just you come in here,' she said, and led Basil into the room where it was obvious that the lady and her old man did pretty well everything.

'Look at that,' she said proudly. 'Going for the sanitary, I am.'

Basil did not stay to look. He only knew that he would be sick if he stayed another moment.

'An excellent idea,' he said and fled.

On the whole, he did not do so badly in his first week, managing to collect just over half the rent which was due. He had to hand in the cash each evening or, if he was late – as often – put it in the night safe of his employers' bank. After he had been working for a fortnight, the secretary spoke to him.

'Mr Merridew,' he said. 'We're not a charitable institution. On the contrary, we're supposed to be a profit-making concern. Our shareholders want to make money, so that they can eat and drink and clothe themselves in comfort.'

'Very natural,' said Basil. 'I sympathise.'

'You'll sympathise a good deal more when you're out on your ear,' said the secretary. 'If I send you to collect £50 rent, I don't expect you to come back with £26. 10s. 0d. and a weary smile. You needn't in fact bother to smile at all and it's also entirely your own affair whether you're weary. The Company's not concerned with that. What we want is the money. Perhaps you haven't understood that so far. You're sure you're not collecting from Mr Brown and paying it out again to Mr Jones?'

'I can't recollect having done that up to date.'

'I'm glad to hear it. Now please understand this. You are not to listen to hard luck stories or anything like that. You're not a County Court judge, understand. That's their job – to keep the wicked landlord from grinding the faces of the poor. Now, you're the wicked landlord, understand,

128

and your job is to grind those faces, see? I don't mind what you say to them. You can use soft soap or threats or whatever you like, but you come back with the rent. Do I make myself quite plain?'

'What am I to do when they say they haven't got it? I can't drag it out of them.'

'Can't you indeed? Of course you can. Look round and see if they've a television set. Half the people who don't pay have one. That's the one thing that gets a County Court judge. He probably hasn't got one himself. "A television set, did you say?" he asks. "Getting a television set before paying your landlord? This is outrageous. Oh, yes, I know it's on the hire purchase system, but you could have paid your rent with the instalments." You can take them to Court with a reasonable chance of getting a good order. Of course, they haven't all got television sets. You must think of something else for the ones it isn't worth taking to Court. Say you'll put the bailiffs in – say you'll do anything which they don't know you can't do – only get the rent – get the rent – get the rent.'

One evening about 8 p.m., when Basil had made his last call, a man came up to him and asked for a light. He was just giving it to him, when he remembered the warning about bag snatchers. He gripped his bag tightly and looked round to see if there were any suspicious-looking characters near. There were. Everyone – except a woman with a baby – looked extremely sinister. 'Thanks, mate,' said the man and walked on. Basil relaxed and made his way home. As usual he was worn out.

'How have you done today, darling?' said Elizabeth.

'Give me a drink. I'm dead.'

'So sorry, darling, we've just finished the bottle. We hoped your commission would buy us another. Will it?'

'It's really too bad,' said Basil; 'here am I slaving away to keep you all and you can't even save me a drink. Really – I thought better of you.'

'Old boy,' said Nicholas, 'I feel very much ashamed. Here's luck,' he added as he finished his drink.

'Now, look here,' said Basil, 'a joke's a joke, but I've had about enough of this. Why should I do all the work? It's time all of you started.'

'But what can I do, old boy?'

'You can have my job.'

'Oh – I'd be no good at it.'

'We think you're wonderful,' said Elizabeth.

'You can go and be a secretary,' said Basil.

The next day Basil set off as usual but had rather more than his previous success. By 8.30 p.m. he had collected the best part of £50. He was quite pleased with himself and felt the triumph of achievement. If he had been asked two months before whether the collection of £50 from about sixty weekly tenants would have given him pleasure, he would have laughed at the idea. But now, tired as he was, he really did feel he had done something. He even hummed a little tune and his vivid imagination soon made him managing director of the Company. He was awakened out of this pleasant daydream by someone snatching his bag from him and running off with it.

'Stop,' he shouted, as soon as he had recovered from the shock. 'Stop thief.' He gave chase, but it was useless. The man had disappeared. Sadly he made his way to the nearest police station, reported the loss and returned home. Next morning, he went straight to the office to tell the secretary. He found that he was engaged.

'I think he wants to speak to you,' said one of the clerks. 'He has two gentlemen with him at the moment.'

A quarter of an hour afterwards, Basil was asked to go into the secretary's room.

'This is a nice business,' said the secretary.

'I'm very sorry,' said Basil.

'These are two police officers who would like to ask you some questions.'

'Certainly,' said Basil, and then he noticed that the face of one of them seemed familiar.

'Good morning, Mr Merridew, I think we've met before.'

'Yes – I seem to remember your face.'

'I was once stationed at Poppleton. You had an unfortunate burglary, you may remember.'

Basil did remember. This was Inspector Larch to whom he had been particularly unpleasant.

'I trust,' said the inspector, 'that you didn't lose any stamps this time as well.'

'No, just the rent,' said Basil, not very happily. He had a perfectly clear conscience about the rent. The burglary was a different matter.

'Well, that's something,' said the inspector. 'Now, perhaps you can give some more details. Could you recognise the man who snatched the bag?'

'I'm afraid not.'

'Dear, dear. Was anyone else in the street when it happened?'

'I don't know.'

'How unfortunate. Which way did the man go?'

'Well – he just ran to the end of the street – which wasn't far – turned right and, when I got to the turning, he'd disappeared.'

'Not much to go on so far. How much was in the bag?'

'Nearly £50.'

'About the usual amount?'

'Rather more. I'd had a good day.'

'Tell me,' said the inspector, 'you don't happen to be short of money yourself, do you?'

'What has that to do with it?'

'Would you mind answering the question first and then I'll tell you what it has to do with it.'

'Well – I have been rather short.'

'How very unfortunate. Now, I'll tell you why I asked you, Mr Merridew. Please understand that we aren't making the slightest suggestion against you, but you'll appreciate that when a robbery like this – or shall we say a loss like this – takes place, we have to consider all the possibilities. It's our duty, you see.'

'Well?'

'Now, if you'll look at it from our point of view, what are the established facts?'

'That my bag containing £50 was snatched from me.'

'I said from our point of view. We only know that £50 is missing. We didn't see it snatched.'

'Surely you accept my word.'

'We accept nothing that isn't proved or self-evident. From our point of view, the loss is due to one of two causes.'

'You mean I may have taken the money myself?'

'Now, I'm not suggesting for a moment that you have.'

'I wish you would,' said Basil. 'The residents of Tapworth Magna paid me £10,000 for that sort of thing.'

'Ah, but they had no right or duty to speak as they did. I have a duty to investigate this loss, and we do find from time to time that rent collectors invent stories of having their bags snatched – particularly when they're short of money.'

'Indeed?'

'Yes. So the first thing I propose to do with your co-operation is to eliminate or establish that possibility in this case.'

'Well, I don't see how I can help you beyond repeating that someone snatched the bag from me.'

'You will. What we often find in these cases is that the bag is thrown away empty quite near the place where it was said to be snatched, and that the rent collector has an unusual amount of money. You will be interested to know that the bag has already been recovered. A constable brought it in last night.'

'Most interesting,' said Basil. 'Now I suppose you'd like to know how much money I have on me?'

'I should.'

'Well, it's £1 odd, if you want to know. Would you like to search me?'

'I would.'

Basil immediately regretted the offer. Having made it, he couldn't very well withdraw it. So he had to submit to the indignity. When it was over, the inspector said, 'We don't always find the money on the rent collector. He may have it at home. Would you mind my coming to your residence?'

Basil hesitated.

'You see, it's to your own advantage, Mr Merridew. Once we've satisfied ourselves about you, you'll have nothing to worry about. How much cash have you at home, may I ask?'

'A few pounds,' said Basil.

'As much as £10 or so?'

'No, more like three or four.'

'Very well, then, if you're willing, Sergeant Kelly and I will accompany you home and confirm what you say.'

'Oh, very well,' said Basil, 'but it's going to make me very late with my rounds today.'

'Too bad,' said the inspector. He hadn't great hopes of being able to arrest Basil, but it was quite pleasant to be able to move him about a bit and there was always the chance that he might be able to prove he'd taken the money himself.

'I've a car outside,' he said.

'How convenient,' said Basil. They entered the car and were driven first of all to the police station.

'If you'll excuse me for a few minutes, I've one or two things to do,' the inspector said.

After an hour and a half of waiting, they left the police station for Basil's flat. No one was in.

'Now, have you any safe or cash box or the like where you keep any loose money?'

'No,' said Basil, 'we seldom have any.'

'I see a cash box on that desk,' said the inspector. 'D'you mind if I look in it?'

Basil saw the cash box with a little surprise. It was an old one which he hadn't used for some time and it wasn't normally on the desk.

'You can look in that with pleasure,' he said. 'Or in anything else. It's not locked.'

The inspector took up the cash box and tried to open it without success.

'It seems to me to be locked,' he said. 'Will you try?' and he handed it to Basil.

It was locked. Basil was again surprised. 'There should be a key in that drawer,' he said, 'but I really don't know why it's locked.'

The inspector opened the drawer, found the key and opened the cash box.

'Well, well,' he said, 'I think it was very wise to keep it locked.'

Inside was a large number of one-pound notes.

Basil appeared genuinely amazed.

'I never put them there,' he said.

'I must warn you,' said the inspector, after he had counted the notes and found them to total £48, 'that anything further you say will be taken down in writing and may be given in evidence if you are charged with an offence. Now, would you like to explain how that money comes to be there?'

'I've no idea,' said Basil. 'It's most extraordinary. I can only imagine my wife has put them there, but for the life of me I can't think where she got them.'

'It's very unfortunate for you, Mr Merridew,' said the inspector. 'I hate coincidences and you must admit it's very strange that you should have about £50 stolen by a man you can't identify and that I should find £50 at your flat of which you say you know nothing. It's particularly queer that this should happen to a gentleman who has had the misfortune to be robbed on a previous occasion by an unidentifiable thief. Are you sure you've nothing more you'd like to say? Sometimes, you know, if a man's charged with an offence, he gets off better when we're able to say that he rendered us every assistance.'

'Well, haven't I given you every assistance?'

'You have given us considerable assistance, I will say that; but not what I would call all possible assistance.'

'What more can I do?'

'Well – if you told us how you came to do it or something of that sort, it would help us even more.'

'I didn't come to do anything. I've no idea how the money came to be there, but I'm sure my wife will be able to explain.'

'Where is she now?'

'I've no idea but she'll probably be back by lunch-time.'

'D'you mind, then, if we wait for her?'

'I've got my rounds to do. I shan't finish by midnight at this rate.'

'Too bad, but it's nicer here than at the police station.'

'Are you proposing to arrest me?'

'I haven't made up my mind yet. I'd prefer to wait for your wife. You say she'll be able to explain the money.'

'Oh, very well,' said Basil.

An hour later Elizabeth returned. 'Oh – that,' she said, when asked for an explanation, 'that's a surprise. I sold the small Rembrandt etching this morning.'

'To whom, may I ask?' said the inspector.

Elizabeth gave the name and address of the dealer and they all went straight to his shop. The inspector was not pleased to find Elizabeth's story duly confirmed, but he made the best of a bad job by saying very brightly to Basil: 'Well, thank you very much, sir. Very much obliged for your help. You'll be able to start on your rounds now, won't you?'

Dreams are curious things. Sometimes, perhaps more usually, you are taking an active part in the incidents, but sometimes you are simply a spectator. Basil's dream was divided into two parts. The first part has just been described; in the second he watched the adventures of Elizabeth. This is what he saw.

'I'm going for an interview,' she announced proudly one day.

'For what?'

'I've applied for the job of secretary to a barrister.'

'But what d'you know about a job like that?'

'Nothing yet, but I can type about forty words a minute and I once did a very little shorthand. I'll get by – with luck.'

The next day she attended Mr Gilbert Munton's chambers in the Temple. Mr Munton was a very busy junior. He was earning about £10,000 a year and had extremely little leisure. A great deal of his work consisted in the drafting of important legal documents. He did not care to dictate and used to write them out in long hand. Then they would be typed out by one of the clerks. As his practice increased, however, he found that he had enough work to keep one typist busy and he eventually decided to have a whole-time secretary. His wife, Mildred, was not at all pleased at the idea. She was extremely possessive and she imagined that all secretaries in real life were like the beauties that are usually seen on the films.

'Why can't you have a dictaphone?' she said.

'I can,' he replied, 'but I should still need a secretary to type the stuff I dictated. I don't know why I haven't had one before. She may be quite useful to you too.'

Gilbert Munton dealt with his wife's jealousy by pretending to her and everyone else – and, it may be, even to himself sometimes – that it did not exist.

'I'm seeing some today,' he added. 'I hope I find a pretty one. I'd hate to have to look at someone plain.'

The same day Mr Munton interviewed three applicants. The first two were obviously efficient and even more obviously unattractive. Mr Munton said he would let them know. He was not at all a bad husband and seldom gave his wife genuine cause for jealousy, but he meant it when he said he wanted a pretty one. He, too, had been to the films and he did not see why, if he had to have a secretary, he shouldn't make the best of it. The third applicant was Elizabeth. She took his breath away. As soon as she came in, he knew that he was bound to engage her. He went through the formalities of asking her a few questions and giving her a short test. She answered the questions beautifully and failed hopelessly in the test – that is to say, she would have failed if Mr Munton had paid the slightest attention to it. But he was only paying attention to her lovely face, her attractive voice and her beautiful legs, of which she showed him just too little, as she sat murmuring in an armchair.

'Now, about salary,' he said. 'I don't suppose we shall fall out over that. How much are you asking?'

'Oh, about fifteen pounds or so,' said Elizabeth.

This was considerably more than Mr Munton had intended to pay but he did not feel that he could even attempt to bargain with this gorgeous creature. 'Very well,' he said, 'shall we say £16?'

'Certainly,' said Elizabeth and added, 'for a start.'

They then chatted about other matters and finally Elizabeth asked when she was to begin.

'At once, if you can.'

'I'd love to. I'm sure I shall enjoy it. It sounds most exciting. Will I be able to come to Court with you?'

It had not been Mr Munton's idea that his secretary should come to Court with him. Her job was to sit in chambers and type out his numerous opinions and other legal documents.

'I expect so,' he answered, 'but how about celebrating your engagement by coming and having some lunch?'

In the normal way Mr Munton's lunch – if he had any at all – was hurriedly eaten at the Inner Temple hall well within half an hour. On this occasion he was not in Court, he told his clerk to postpone three conferences and he took Elizabeth out for a lunch which lasted two hours.

'I think I'm going to enjoy this job,' she said.

The next day Mr Munton was in Court and Elizabeth came over to watch him. At the end of the day she said to him on their return to chambers: 'I think you were wonderful. I wish I had a case. I'd have you to appear for me. The way the judge listens to you – you must be awfully important.'

'Oh, well,' he said modestly but pleased, 'I've been at it a long time.' Then he added, in a slightly embarrassed tone: 'I say, I suppose you haven't been able to type out any of those pleadings?'

'I've been terribly naughty,' said Elizabeth, 'but I was so enthralled by your case I couldn't tear myself away. I'd get on with some now but I want to go and meet a girl friend for tea. That'll be all right, won't it?'

'Oh – certainly. Will you be back again this evening?'

'Well,' said Elizabeth, 'if you'd like me to stay on late, I could get some dinner somewhere no doubt.'

A few minutes later Mr Munton was explaining to his wife that he'd have to work late at chambers and would not be in to dinner.

'Have you engaged a secretary?' his wife asked.

'I'm not sure,' he lied; 'none of the ones today were very satisfactory. I may have to give one of them a trial.'

'What does she look like?'

Normally Mr Munton would have replied cheerfully, 'A beauty', but on this occasion he felt a little uncomfortable about it.

'Oh – so-so,' he said.

That evening very little legal work was done by Elizabeth or Mr Munton but the dinner was very pleasant. The next day Elizabeth came to Court again and spent the whole time there. On their return, Mr Munton asked tentatively about the documents his clients were waiting for.

'Oh, don't worry,' said Elizabeth, 'I've had a brilliant idea.'

'What is it?'

'Wait and see.'

They couldn't have dinner again the next night though Elizabeth made Mr Munton feel he was treating her rather badly by not suggesting it. The whole of the following day was again spent by Elizabeth in Court and Mr Munton began to become really worried about the typing. It had got to be done, however beautiful Elizabeth was. To his amazement, on his return to chambers it was all there waiting for him.

'But you're a marvel,' he said; 'when did you do all this?'

'After I left chambers last night.'

'But I can't let you do all this work at home.'

'Oh – I didn't. I just took it to the stationers. They do it so much better than I can, and it can come out of the petty cash. What with income tax and surtax, it won't make any real difference to you.'

Thereafter, for a time Elizabeth's legal work for Mr Munton consisted in carrying his manuscripts to the stationers and fetching them back when they were typed. She soon found, however, that there was no reason why one of the clerks shouldn't do this. It was astonishing, however, how often Mr Munton required her services late at night.

For a long time those services consisted simply in dining and chatting, but with women like Elizabeth and men like Mr Munton things can't go on just like that for ever. The dreadful night came when Basil (in his dream), unable to move or say a word, saw Elizabeth and Mr Munton, after a very good dinner and plenty of champagne, take a room in a hotel, go into it and start to prepare for a night of rapture. (Mrs Munton was away for the weekend.) As Basil watched the performance drawing to its inevitable conclusion, he was snoring loudly and finally he woke up with a start. He looked extremely ill. As he woke up, indeed perhaps the cause of his doing so, Nicholas burst into the room.

'I say, old man, I've got it,' he half shouted. 'I've had the most splendid idea. You go to a solicitor and – good heavens, what's the matter? – you're white as a sheet.'

'I've had the most terrible dream, old boy.'

'I should say you have. You look awful. What was it?'

'I dreamed, old man,' said Basil slowly, 'I dreamed – it was too ghastly – I dreamed I had to go to work. Just fancy – me a rent collector.'

Prize Story

'Ghosts, no,' he said, 'but poltergeists, yes. Oh, definitely, yes.'

'Well,' I said, 'I disbelieve in nothing, but I've never had any evidence of their existence yet.'

'Haven't you indeed?' he said. 'Well, sit down and listen to this – if you've the time.'

I had, and I sat.

'Let me see,' he went on, 'it was about ten years ago. You were out of the country then, I believe. 1957, '58. The Premium Bond affair.' He chuckled.

'You probably don't know anything about Premium Bonds, but you don't need to know much to understand this story. Each month there was a draw but only the lucky numbers were published, not the names of the owners. Well, on the 1st June 1957 they had the first draw and one of the lucky numbers to win a top prize of £1,000 was 1 KP 685771. We'll call the owner Mr Brown. No one but the authorities and Mr Brown and anyone he chose to tell knew of his good fortune. Well – he was just lucky. So were a number of other people. There was nothing odd at that stage about 1 KP 685771.

'But next month – the lst July 1957 – there was another draw. Even if you'd already won with a bond, your bond still went into the draw, unless you withdrew it yourself or died. Mr Brown let his lucky number have another chance, and, when the winning numbers were published after the July draw, would you believe it? 1 KP 685771 was drawn again for £1,000.

'Naturally on this occasion the newspapers commented on Mr Brown's phenomenal luck, though of course they still didn't know who he was. And there actually appeared in the personal column of *The Times* an advertisement from a box number to this effect: "Gambler will pay for a 50% share in 1 KP 685771".

'August came and another draw and blow me down if 1 KP 685771 didn't draw another £1,000. Well – that was too much of a good thing for the public. Once lucky was difficult enough, twice in succession was phenomenal, but three times – well, there was something odd about it. Letters to this effect began to appear in the popular press and even *The Times* published a well written suggestion that, to allay public anxiety on the subject, would it not be better if the Postmaster-General looked into the matter?

'The Postmaster-General remained quite unmoved, knowing perfectly well that the clamour would die down after two or three more draws in which 1 KP 685771 did not figure. So he waited quite happily until the September draw. The Postmaster-General was a courageous man, quite used to meeting danger without flinching but even he went white when 1 KP 685771 drew another £1,000 on the 1st September. He was unable to act before the Press and most of the House of Commons assailed him. But in reply he said at once that he was having the machine examined immediately by an independent scientist of unquestioned ability and integrity – who, he hastened to add, was not interested in 1 KP 685771.

'The public waited for the result of the examination almost as they do for the birth of a Royal baby. At last the bulletin was issued: "I have examined the machine in question exhaustively and I hereby certify that it is in perfect working order and has no bias in favour of 1 KP 685771. Signed, etc." In reply to questions in the House the Minister said that he could add to the certificate that out of 50 complete dress rehearsals made after Sir Torquemada Twist's full examination the number 1 KP 685771 had not turned up once. Nor indeed had any of the series 1 KP. "So that," he added, "had any of these tests been the actual draw for next month 1 KP 685771 would not have been drawn."

'The public mumbled something and waited for the next draw. There were all sorts of important national and international affairs on at that time but even *The Times* had on the top right-hand corner of its outside sheet the words: "Same again", when the October draw awarded another £1,000 to the owner of the incredibly lucky number. "Incredibly" is the right word. No certificate from all the scientists in the world could now satisfy the public and, in response to almost universal public demand, the machine was changed for one of a completely different pattern which was almost guaranteed by its makers not to throw up 1 KP 685771. Of course they couldn't properly exclude that number from any possibility of turning up. That would have been a fraud on the holder of the bond. But they actually had 1,000 test draws and assured the public that the nauseating number which everyone now knew by heart, and which had become a comedian's joke, had not appeared on any one of those draws – nor, indeed, had any number anywhere near it.

'The public sighed with relief and waited for the next draw. It was not simply that they felt that Mr Brown was having more than was good for him. Most people don't normally resent other people's good fortune. It was the very real fear that if the machine had a bias *in favour* of one number, it might have a bias against *another*, and that you might be sitting there with your 10 premium bonds in blissful ignorance of the fact that none of them had a chance.

'However, now there was a new machine. In spite of that, "Gambler" raised his offer for half the ticket to £100. He would have done very well if it had been accepted. You could almost hear a loud whistle rise from the country as a whole when the papers published the result of the draw. The November draw had brought another £1,000 for 1 KP 685771.

'Suddenly the public became angry. Angry at its own stupidity. Of course it wasn't the machine. Of course the machine worked perfectly fairly when operated by Sir Torquemada Twist. It was one or more of the people operating the machine. It was a swindle. In vain did the Postmaster-General state that all the personnel concerned were persons of the utmost probity and that none of them held premium bonds. "They may not," said the public, "but their sisters or their cousins or close personal friends may." "Even if it's not a fraud," wrote one angry man, "it shows they're operating the machine carelessly to let one chap win it every time."

'The matter had now assumed serious proportions, for once the public suspected that there was something wrong with the draw – even though it only favoured one person to the tune of £1,000 a month and even though the difference to the remaining bondholders as a whole was negligible – the premium bond scheme would be doomed to failure. The Government had to act, and did. They installed yet a third machine and they had it certified and locked by Sir Torquemada, and guarded by a company of Grenadiers from the time Sir Torquemada had locked it up until the time of the next draw. The keys were kept personally by the Permanent Secretary to the Treasury. On the day of the next draw – it was now December – the Lord Chancellor and the Lord Chief Justice, together with the heads of some of the other professions, attended the draw and the Lord Chancellor himself was handed the key by the Permanent Secretary to the Treasury. Nothing could go wrong this time.

'The machine was set in motion. Its principle was much the same as the roulette wheel. A huge board contained slots with the numbers which were required to make up the serial numbers of a bond. Then, when a lever was pressed, a sufficient number of balls was released and, after being whirled round the board many times by a mechanical device, they eventually found their way into the numbered slots. Another device showed the order in which the numbers were to be read. There were similar devices for the letters. The machine was started as many times as there were prizes. One by one the balls sped their way into the slots. The Press were present in full strength and a number of ordinary members of the public. When the first three balls in one throw of the machine went into 6, 7, 7 there was a slight gasp, but the other numbers on that occasion were not 8, 5 and 1. The draw went on and the Lord Chancellor and the Lord Chief Justice became drowsier and drowsier. They each had reserved judgments to deliver and were thinking of them rather than of the silly little balls they were watching. They were shaken out of their dreams by a shout – a unanimous shout – led by the Presidents of Lloyd's and the Royal College of Surgeons. 1 KP 685771 had turned up again – and on the very last throw.

'It was impossible but it had happened. The results were what you might expect. "Gambler" increased his offer for a half share in the bond to £5,000 and the public insisted on a new machine and new operators. The result was the same in the next draw. The ridiculous position now was that, instead of people not expecting it possible for the number to turn up, it seemed impossible that it should not do so. January, February, March, the tale was the same, but before the April draw Mr Brown, whoever he was, sold to Mr "Gambler" a half share for £10,000. The latter must have waited for the draw on the 1st April with more than usual interest. Everyone else was extremely interested but not as much as he. The day arrived, the soldiers and detectives made way for the distinguished gathering of what might be called umpires, and eventually the machine was set in motion. For the first time in the history of the Premium Bond draw 1 KP 685771 did not even receive a mention, and it never did again. Mr "Gambler" became sadder but not wiser, Mr Brown remained if not wiser, certainly no sadder.

'Well, there you are. There's my story. Only a poltergeist could have done it. It obviously liked Mr Brown, but would have nothing to do with Mr "Gambler". Perhaps it disapproved of gambling, though obviously it was broad-minded up to a point. Well – does that convince you?'

I thought for a moment.

'No,' I said, after a short pause. 'It doesn't. I can think of a much simpler explanation than a poltergeist.'

'Indeed,' he said, 'and what is it, may I ask?'

'The story isn't true. You made it up.'

He hesitated for a moment and then said: 'Well, as a matter of fact, you're right – but, if it had happened, it would have had to have been a poltergeist, wouldn't it?'

Proof

The pompous self-satisfied little lawyer from London had been holding forth the whole evening and I had tried in vain to deflate him. Not merely were my efforts wasted but he turned his batteries in my direction and effectually silenced me. I prayed for reinforcements. It may surprise you to know that, although I come from a long line of distinguished lawyers, I have a particular aversion to the breed. This may be due to the fact that, whereas my ancestors for over 150 years back were nearly all eminent judges, I was unable to satisfy the examiners in Roman Law and so had never even achieved the distinction of being called to the Bar. Be that as it may, I had an instinctive dislike of lawyers. This one was a particularly odious specimen, and I disliked him all the more because everyone else seemed interested in what he had to say and he was allowed virtually to monopolise the conversation.

We had been sitting in the bar of the small Lakeland hotel where I had been spending a much-needed holiday. Since my failure at law I had been employed in many capacities, including that of clerk, salesman and commercial traveller. At the moment, I was going up and down the country trying to sell the publications of a new psychical research society. As my earnings were entirely dependent on what I sold, I had a hard time of it to make a living, trying to persuade very matter-of-fact earthy people to buy our books on psychic phenomena. How I wished that some manifestation would present itself to the busy little lawyer and reduce his self-esteem, but nothing happened.

On and on he went and it was a great relief to me when two strangers suddenly came in and distracted everyone's attention from him. They were very ordinary-looking people, but they entered with some noise and, as their faces were unknown to any of us, their entrance automatically stopped the conversation. They walked straight up to the bar, ordered a pint of beer each and drank it without a word. That done, they repeated the dose and only then did they seem to relax. Finally, one said to the other: 'That was a complete and utter waste of time.'

'Absolutely.'

'D'you know,' said the first, addressing us generally, 'we've been all the way to the top of Grimstone Crag, and we didn't see a thing.'

They could not have been ordinary climbers, as no climber would consider any climb a waste of time, view or no view. Accordingly, none of us was much impressed and I was afraid that the little lawyer would soon be holding forth again. However, after the second stranger had said: 'Terrible waste of time. Hours of solid climbing and nothing to show for it except a thirst,' a small man at the end of the bar, whom I had not previously noticed, said:

'You don't know what a waste of time is.'

Everyone turned towards the speaker.

'Waste of time,' he repeated. 'Let me tell you of a waste of time which will make you feel that every moment of your climb was well spent.'

Without waiting for an invitation to proceed, he went on: 'It was a good many years ago and it happened in these parts. A detective was trailing a badly wanted criminal. He had almost caught up with him when the fellow went off into the mountains at night. It was moonlight and the detective, who was dead keen, went after him. By luck he sighted him against the sky and, after a scrambling climb, at last he got within hailing distance and called on the man to surrender. As he did so, the detective slipped and eventually found himself, by the mercy of God, with a sprained or broken ankle on a slightly projecting ledge. Below, a drop of hundreds of feet; above, almost sheer. He regretted his hasty pursuit and was wondering whether and when he would be rescued when he heard the criminal hailing him.

' "Hallo, there," said the criminal, "I'll go and get a rope."

'The detective said nothing for a moment and then he shouted: "Are you William Turner?"

' "Certainly."

' "I have a warrant for your arrest for the murder of Sidney Blunt."

' "Well, what are you going to do about it?" asked Turner.

' "You're under arrest now," said the detective.

' "Doesn't feel like it," said Turner.

' "Now, look here," said the detective, "I naturally want to get out of here but I can't let you haul me out without telling you that I shall arrest you as soon as you do." It will be seen that the detective had a peculiarly high standard of morals.

' "Oh, shut up," said the criminal, whose morals were – except for the little matter of the murder – equally high. "I'm going for a rope," and he went away.

'Hours later he returned, when the detective had almost given him up. It had come on to rain during the night and rained incessantly next day, and no one had come into his sight since Turner left.

150

' "You still alive?" shouted Turner. "I don't want to waste my time if you're not."

' "Yes," shouted the detective.

' "I'm afraid I'm by myself," said Turner, "but you'll understand that, in the circumstances." The detective did understand, but he began to wonder how he could be rescued by one man alone – even with a rope.

' "You'll have to wait a bit," said Turner, and began to make the descent.

'I won't describe the difficulties to experts like you gentlemen,' said the speaker, 'but you may take it that even you would have found it a tough proposition. As it was, neither Turner nor the detective were real climbers and it was remarkable that Turner was able to reach the detective at all. However, after some time, he did so and threw one end of the rope to him. Now, whether the detective's ankle was broken or only sprained doesn't very much matter. You can perhaps visualise the appalling nature of their attempt to climb to safety. It required every ounce of strength and nerve each of them possessed. However, at long – very long – last their almost superhuman efforts (very different, I may say, from those needed for the little stroll you two gentlemen have just taken) were rewarded and they got to safety and stood looking at each other. The detective almost fainted as a result of the pain and exertion, but he just had enough strength to say: "Thank you. I'm sorry ..." and, with the last words, to aim a blow at Turner's jaw with the idea of knocking him out. He had, of course, realised that, unless he could do this, Turner would make good his escape. He had warned him that he would arrest him and, like a good detective, he felt bound to do so if he could. Unfortunately he had wholly insufficient strength to carry out his purpose and, as Turner avoided the blow, the detective lurched sideways and fell over the edge. As he was still roped to Turner, the latter was carried after him and they crashed to death hundreds of feet below. And you two gentlemen talk of a waste of time." '

'Very interesting,' piped up the lawyer and, once again, attention was focused on him. 'But d'you suggest that story is true?'

'Absolutely,' said the small man gravely.

'Now, gentlemen,' said the lawyer, 'I think I can demonstrate to you conclusively that our friend here has been pulling your legs. The story can't be true.' He paused and took the middle of the floor. 'Now, sir,' he went on, 'did I rightly understand you to infer that there were no witnesses of this accident?'

'Quite,' said the small man.

'Did both men die instantaneously?'

'Quite.'

'Then,' said the lawyer, 'as no one saw them die and as they could have told their story to no one, you couldn't possibly know that it happened as you have told us.'

He paused and gazed in triumph round his audience.

'Unless, of course,' he added facetiously, 'you chance to be the ghost of one of the men.'

'Quite,' said the small man and vanished.

Striking the Balance

'My Lord,' says the foreman of the jury, 'one of the jury has met the prisoner.' 'Very proper of you to tell me,' says the judge. 'The juryman in question had better stand down.' At the same time in another Court the judge is informing counsel on both sides that he holds fifty £1 shares in a big public company which is a party to the case in front of him. 'Does anyone object?' 'Oh no, my Lord, no one has the least objection.' 'I thought I had better tell you,' says the judge.

These are typical examples which show how careful both judge and jury are to see that their reputation for integrity remains as high as it is. And it is very high. Litigants and criminals may complain of this and that judge, they may describe him in all sorts of terms, but they never suggest that he is even capable of corruption. They never suggest that a jury or one or more of its members has been bribed. Justice in England may be slow and expensive, it may even make mistakes, but it is pure.

Or so everyone has always thought. But their ideas were rudely shaken by the case of Tommy Newcastle. Very rudely shaken indeed. Tommy had been a solicitor's clerk in an office which specialised in criminal work. Unfortunately there was some disagreement between Tommy and his employers about some cash which disappeared, and Tommy found himself without a job.

Not long afterwards, he wandered down to one of his regular haunts, the Old Bailey. He listened to a case or two and then came out into the lobby for some air. On one of the seats he saw a woman sitting crying. Tommy was a sympathetic person and he walked over to her and asked what was the matter. Not that he had to be told. Obviously, her husband or boyfriend or someone of whom she was fond had gone inside or was on the way there. He was quite right. A case of receiving. Tommy asked her to tell him all about it. She told him, and added at the end that what made it so awful was that he'd four previous convictions for the same thing. He'd get a stretch this time and no mistake. And there was another baby on the way. What was she to do? He was a good husband when he was at home – which, through no wish of his, had not been very often in the last twelve years. Tommy considered the matter.

'How much did he get for the stuff?' he asked. 'I mean,' he added hastily, 'how much did they say he got for it?'

'£200 – for what they traced.'

'Humph,' said Tommy. 'And how much was the stuff they didn't trace worth?'

'I wouldn't rightly know,' said the woman, 'but what difference would it make if I did?'

'Not much really,' said Tommy. 'I was just interested. Now look,' he added, after a moment or two's thought. 'Don't you say anything to anyone, but I may be able to help. Which Court is he being tried in?'

The woman told him.

'Old Turnip-Top,' said Tommy. 'I see.' He paused again. Then: 'You know,' he went on, 'a bit of help from a judge in his summing-up, or one juryman on your side, can make a heap of difference.'

'What do you mean?' asked the woman. She also believed in the incorruptibility of justice.

'I've known cases,' said Tommy, 'where at the start it was eleven to one on the jury for guilty or not guilty and the one has persuaded the other eleven to change their minds. Of course, when you get two strong-minded people on a jury, who don't see eye to eye, there's a disagreement. But that doesn't often happen. Usually there's not more than one, and the jury vote the way he thinks. Of course, sometimes there isn't one, and then anything may happen – unless you can make one of them strong-minded. And as for a judge's summing-up, well, if you've been here before, I don't have to tell you about that.'

'But they always seem to tell the jury to convict. When my old man's in the dock, anyway.'

'Maybe,' said Tommy, 'but if he said the other thing, they'd let him off, wouldn't they?'

'I suppose so. But how can you help?'

'Never you mind,' said Tommy. 'And don't you say a word to your husband about it – not till afterwards, anyway. You just let the trial take its course. You're sure he's in old Turnip-Top's court? I'd better make quite certain.'

He went and looked on the list.

'Yes, that's right enough,' he said, 'as long as there's not a transfer. Now I'm going off. Remember, not a word to a soul. Give me your address and I'll come to tea the day after tomorrow – with you *both*.'

'I don't know how to thank you,' said the woman.

'Don't try,' said Tommy, 'till the day after tomorrow.' The day after tomorrow came and the tea party took place. Mr Wilkins, the receiver, could hardly believe his ears when the jury said 'Not guilty,' and the judge said 'You're discharged.' But he didn't waste any time in the dock wondering – in case the jury changed their minds. He and his wife were back home as soon as they could get there. And they gave Tommy the tea of his life. Whisky and gin mostly. And £25.

'Sure you can afford it?' said Tommy.

'We can't ever thank you enough,' said the woman, who was fond of her husband and liked him about the place.

'Make it £30, Alf,' she added, and they did.

It was not long after this that Alf recommended Tommy to a friend who was in a similar line of business and had also got into difficulties. Tommy promised to see him. They met at Marble Arch – the friend was on bail – and Tommy heard all about it in the Park. He also asked him a few questions about the case and then said: 'Where are you coming up?'

'Sessions.'

'Sessions, eh? That's not so easy. But I'll think about it.'

He thought for a minute. His companion became anxious.

'It's worth £50 to you,' he said.

'Now look,' said Tommy, 'don't get me wrong. I like helping people out but I don't ask anything for it. If you like to give me a present afterwards that's up to you.'

'Make it £75,' said the man.

'I don't know that it can be done at all,' said Tommy.

'£80.'

'That's not it,' said Tommy. 'I've got to know which Court it's in first.'

'£100,' urged his companion.

'I'll meet you there,' said Tommy, 'before you surrender, and then I'll tell you if it can be done. If it's in Long John Silver's Court I doubt if I can do a thing. But let's hope it isn't.'

It wasn't, and just before he surrendered to his bail, the prisoner was delighted to receive a confident wink and nod from Tommy. All the same he didn't feel at all good in the dock. With warders behind and a judge in front and everything very formal and precise and the cells downstairs. But three hours later he could have kissed Tommy. He was free. He gave Tommy £125, he was so pleased. And, he thought, there may always be another time. Just as well to treat him handsome.

It was not long before Tommy's fame began to spread in the underworld. It was a new idea and it seemed to work. And they liked a man who never wanted anything in advance. Of course he was bilked occasionally, but not often. A mixture of genuine gratitude and the possibility of help being wanted in the future kept the takings side well up. But he didn't accept every case.

'Sorry, old man,' he'd say, 'but I got to be careful. Just daren't. Anyway, if I tried it, it's hopeless in that court.'

Most particular Tommy was about the Court where his client was being tried. He had to know the number of the Court and the name of the judge. Occasionally even then things went wrong and his client was convicted. But this was rare and, even when it happened, Tommy did not become too unpopular with the party concerned. After all, he'd had nothing from him.

But, of course, fame such as Tommy's can't go on for long without coming to the ears of the police. At first they took no notice of it. Who'd ever heard of anyone dropping a judge a five-pound note? Or a juryman either. But when Inspector Branch lost his case against Benny Bones things began to happen.

Inspector Branch was not a very clever man but he was as straight as a die. If he brought a case against you, of one thing you could be certain and that was that the evidence was not rigged. You could trust him all the way as far as integrity was concerned. That is why he had got as far as he had, because, although he had just enough intelligence to cope with his job, he was very far from being brilliant.

The inspector had been after Benny Bones for a long time but he'd always slipped through his fingers somehow. Now at last he'd got him. In the inspector's view, it was an open and shut case. Before it came on, he even paid a friendly visit to Benny in the cells. He felt almost sorry for him.

'Cheer up, old boy,' he said, 'you've had a good run.'

'Still running,' said Benny, and winked at him.

The inspector thought nothing of the wink until at lunch-time he happened to notice Tommy coming away from the judge's entrance to the Old Bailey. He didn't think much about it then, but he'd heard of Tommy and he just wondered. But not very much though. It was an open and shut case. At least so he thought. But when Mr Justice Bream began to sum up he started to feel an emptiness inside him and, as the judge went on, the inspector's face actually went pale. And when the judge ended he felt like jumping into the Thames. Although the inspector was not brilliant, he did know the difference between a summing-up for a conviction and a summing up for an acquittal. The former ends something like this with emphasis placed on the appropriate words: 'Of course, if you still have any reasonable doubt in your minds, members of the jury, you will acquit the prisoner, but if you are quite satisfied as to his guilt, you will not let any motives of sympathy either with him or his family come between you and your duty.'

The latter ends something like this: 'Of course, if you are satisfied of the prisoner's guilt you will say so, but if, having regard to all the circumstances you feel some doubt about the matter, then it is the prisoner's right that you should say Not Guilty.'

And that is what the judge said in Benny Bones' case, and the jury, without leaving the box, acquitted him. As he left the dock, Benny gave the inspector another wink.

But the inspector was not taking his defeat lying down. He requested an interview with an Assistant Commissioner of Police and placed the facts before him.

'You're not suggesting, inspector, that Mr Justice Bream was bribed?' said the Assistant Commissioner bluntly.

'I'm not suggesting anything, sir,' said the inspector. 'But you've heard of Tommy Newcastle, and so have I. And I have told you what I saw and heard myself. It seemed to me to be my duty to do so.'

The Assistant Commissioner decided to have Tommy Newcastle watched and he was genuinely surprised at the result. He was not surprised that Tommy was regularly seen hanging about the place where jurymen are to be found, because they go in like the public except when they retire to consider their verdict. But he was surprised to find that Tommy would be seen not only outside the judges' entrance but occasionally outside a judge's house and that on several of these occasions he appeared to be fingering £5 notes. It can't be true, he said to himself, but he spoke to the Commissioner about it.

In consequence of their discussion, Mr Justice Cramp, going one day to the Old Bailey from South Kensington, was surprised to find that, whenever he happened to look round, a man seemed to be following him. The judge liked exercise and walked all the way. When he found the man still behind him near Blackfriars Bridge, he stopped. So did the man. The judge called a uniformed police officer, said who he was, and together they approached the man.

'This gentleman says you've been following him,' said the constable.

The man looked embarrassed, but said nothing.

'Are you deaf?' asked the constable. 'Have you been following this gentleman?'

'Can I have a word with you, mate?' said the man.

The constable had not had the privilege of protecting a judge before. He might give evidence before him one day and judges had a knack of remembering people. So he'd show what he could do.

'There's nothing you need be afraid to say in the presence of this gentleman,' he said, and, as the man still said nothing, he went on more loudly: 'Now, answer me. Have you been following him, or not? You've got a tongue in your head, haven't you?'

'Yes, I have,' said the man eventually.

'And might I know the reason?' asked the judge.

'Yes, and make it snappy,' said the constable.

'I'm a police officer,' said the man not very happily.

'What!' said the judge.

'Oh, you are, are you?' said the constable. 'Let's see your warrant card.'

The man produced it.

'Oh!' said the constable. Nothing he had so far read or learned provided for such a situation. He said nothing and waited for the judge to speak.

'And why are you following me, officer?' he asked.

'Orders, sir,' said the man.

'From whom?'

'Superintendent Dean, sir.'

'And why has Superintendent Dean ordered you to follow me? I haven't asked for protection.'

'No, sir.'

'If there's been a threat against me, why haven't I been told?'

'There's been no threat against you, sir.'

'Then what is it?'

'It's – it's highly confidential, sir.'

'D'you mean that you're not allowed to tell me?' asked the judge.

'I don't think I ought to, sir, without permission. I'm sure you'll understand, sir, that I'm placed in a very embarrassing position.'

'I can see that, but I should like to know what it's all about.'

'What would you like me to do, my Lord?' asked the uniformed policeman.

'Well, you'd better report the matter, constable, and so shall I. In the meantime, I suppose the other police officer had better go on following me, if those are his orders. Hope I don't walk too fast for you.' And the judge walked on.

Mr Justice Cramp was not the only judge to be followed. And when the Lord Chief Justice heard of it, he was furious. He went to see the Home Secretary, the Home Secretary sent for the Commissioner and everyone felt extremely embarrassed. You can't ask a judge if he's been offered a bribe. But there was Tommy fingering his notes and there were the prisoners getting off more often than not. But Tommy was never seen to speak to a juryman or a judge, so they couldn't touch him. It was most worrying. Indeed, one judge gave the jury a searching look and asked them if any of them had spoken about the case to anyone, and threatened them with every kind of penalty if they did. The jury did nothing, except acquit the prisoner as they didn't like the way the judge had spoken to them. Tommy Newcastle had nothing to do with that particular case. But the prisoner thought he had and was most grateful, showing his gratitude in the usual way.

Tommy was now becoming quite affluent and he started to turn business away more often.

One evening he was sitting in his flat reading the paper and sampling a glass of port, when two men called to see him.

'You Tommy Newcastle?'

'I am.'

'Good. We've got a job for you.'

'Oh?'

'Yes – you've read about it, I expect. Jimmy Bellows.'

'Oh, that's murder,' said Tommy. 'I don't touch murder.'

'You touch this one,' said one of the men.

'Oh, no I don't,' said Tommy.

'Now look,' said the second man. 'We came here quite friendly and it'll be worth two-fifty quid for you when you've fixed it.'

'Sorry,' said Tommy, 'can't be done.'

'You let me finish,' said the second man. 'It's two-fifty for you when you've fixed it – but, if you don't, there'll be two murders instead of one. See? And it won't be an easy way out either. Ever seen anyone beaten up with one of these?' and he brought out an ugly-looking knuckle-duster from his pocket.

'Be reasonable,' said Tommy. He was pleading now. 'I can't do it, I tell you.'

'Well, you know what'll happen if you don't. Shan't warn you again. See you after the verdict – one way or another.'

The two men left, and Tommy, really frightened, went to the nearest police station. He asked for police protection, but found it rather embarrassing to explain why.

'Threatened to beat you up and kill you? But why?' Tommy paused. He knew the men meant what they said. He knew the type. So he had rushed round to the police station without first thinking what he was going to tell them.

'Look,' said the inspector who interviewed him, 'you help us and we'll help you. That's fair enough, isn't it?'

'What d'you want?' asked Tommy.

'You're a good bit in the news today, aren't you?' said the inspector. 'If you'll tell us how you do it and who else is in it, we'll give you a guard night and day.'

'Do what?' said Tommy, playing for time.

'You know well enough,' said the inspector. 'And I was about to add vice versa.'

'What are you getting at?'

'Quite simple. If you don't tell us, all we'll do is to catch the merchants who murder you – after they've done it.'

'But you can't just leave a man to be butchered,' said Tommy, getting really alarmed.

'How do we know that it's not just a cock-and-bull story?'

'But I swear it's true.'

'So you do. But why should I believe you? A lot of people swear things, you know. And even if all you say is true, it may have been just bluff.'

'But it wasn't. I know it wasn't.'

'We hear that every day, old man. But I might believe you if you came clean – really clean, I mean. Anyway, it's up to you.'

As Tommy said nothing, the inspector got up and yawned.

'Well,' he said, 'sorry we can't do anything for you. We're short of men. Perhaps you've read about it.'

'All right,' said Tommy, 'I'll tell you. But you'll promise to look after me?'

'We'll look after you,' said the inspector. 'As a matter of fact, I think you're important enough to come to Scotland Yard. Safe enough there. We'll take you in the morning.'

The next day Tommy had the honour of an interview with five highly placed officials at Scotland Yard. He told them of the threats that had been made, and what he'd been asked to do.

'Yes,' said the Assistant Commissioner. 'We'll go into that in a moment. First of all, you tell us how you've been operating.'

'I'll tell you in confidence,' said Tommy.

'There's no such thing as confidence in crime, and I warn you that anything you say may be used in evidence if you're charged hereafter.'

'Look here,' said Tommy, 'I came here for help, not to be threatened.'

'No one's threatening you,' said the Assistant Commissioner, 'but, as you mentioned confidence, I felt it right to warn you. However, as you've nothing to tell us, and we're busy men ...' He stopped in the middle.

'Oh, well,' said Tommy, 'there's nothing for it. But you'll give me protection?'

'If you satisfy us that you've told us the truth, we will.'

'Well – what d'you want to know?' asked Tommy.

'You know quite well what we want to know. What have you been doing in all these cases?'

'Well – nothing wrong,' said Tommy, 'and, to tell you the truth, nothing at all.'

The Assistant Commissioner got up.

'All right,' he said, 'you look after yourself.'

'But I swear I've been doing nothing. I only took on cases where I thought there was a good chance of the man being acquitted. And usually I was right. But, of course, I had to pretend I was doing something, you see. You do believe me, don't you?'

But they didn't, not then nor for some after Tommy was beaten up. Jimmy Bellows' friends left him alive by mistake and then at last a slow piecing together of all the evidence showed that he had told the truth after all, and that all he'd done had been, as he'd said, nothing. But the Bellows case had finished him. He felt sure the man would be convicted. So, if he took it on, they'd think he'd double-crossed them. If he didn't take it on, it was just as bad. There was no way out. The whole story was eventually published in the Press, and British justice was triumphantly vindicated. But the case of Tommy Newcastle had been painful for the public while it lasted, and it remained painful for him for some time afterwards.

The Limit

There was nothing particularly odd about the application itself. It was the consequences of its being granted which staggered people. The judge was Mr Justice Broadbent, a man of seventy-two who could have retired already had he wished to do so but who could stay for another three years if he preferred, until he reached the age limit. He had read science at Oxford and that was one of the grounds for the application.

'My Lord,' said counsel, 'might I mention to your Lordship the case of Tiptree against Anstruther? It's number 374 in the non-jury list. I appear for the plaintiff and my learned friend Mr Boles appears for the defendant and consents to my application.'

'What is the application?' asked the judge.

'My Lord, the case involves among other things the consideration of certain scientific data and both my learned friend and I felt that it would be less of a burden on your Lordship than on most of the other judges in this division. My application is that your Lordship should hear the case.'

'I see,' said the judge. 'What is the nature of the action?'

'Mr Tiptree and Mr Anstruther are neighbours, my Lord, and were at one time also close business associates. Unfortunately they have fallen out and there are various claims and counter-claims. Some of them arise out of their

166

business relationship and it is those which will make it desirable for the tribunal which tries the case to have some knowledge of science. The other matters arise partly out of the fact that they are neighbours, boundary disputes and so forth.'

'Are all these matters to be heard together?'

'My learned friend and I are agreed that, having regard to the fact that these gentlemen are neighbours and live in a small village it is highly desirable that all disputes between them should be decided as quickly as possible and once and for all. I may add that there has been an agreement not to appeal. The parties wish to clear the air. And once that has been done there is reasonable hope that they will both accept the situation, whatever it may be.'

'The case will obviously take some little time,' said the judge.

'Yes, it must,' said counsel. 'That is why I am venturing to mention the matter to your Lordship now.'

The judge thought for a moment.

'Very well,' he said, 'if both parties would like me to try it, I will. We'd better fix a day.'

So a day was fixed three weeks ahead and no one who had heard the application, other than the parties involved, thought any more about it. Applications for a particular judge in the Queen's Bench Division to hear a case on the ground that he has special qualifications for trying it are not very frequent, but there is nothing strange about them.

The case began on the day which had been fixed for it and it did not attract the attention of the Press. It was only when it had been progressing for a fortnight that people began to take a little notice. After it had been going on for two months most people who read *The Times* had heard of it and the whole of the legal profession in London were well aware of it. So was the Lord Chief Justice, because it meant that the time of Mr Justice Broadbent was completely taken up with this one case. There was a shortage of judges and the fact that one of them had to devote all his time to the action was almost as bad as his being ill.

'How long is this confounded case of yours going on for?' the Lord Chief Justice asked the judge.

'If I live to complete it, I shall be lucky. No sooner do I appear to have sewn up one issue very nicely when either some important further evidence is discovered or another issue of even greater length discloses itself. So far I have started to deal with a complicated contract relating to the exploitation of a patent for making certain electrical appliances, a claim for assault, another for trespass and there are claims for libel and slander waiting in the background.'

'But it's ridiculous to have them all tried together.'

The judge explained that both parties wanted it so. 'I must say,' he added, 'that, although there is the bitterest enmity between the two parties, the one thing they both agree upon is that every possible bone of contention shall be dealt with in this action. If one side neglects to call a piece of evidence and subsequently applies to be allowed to do so the other side always accedes to the application. Neither side even suggests that the other side is seeking to delay the trial or to obstruct in any way. But that's the only thing they agree upon. Apart from that, it's a fight to the death and no holds barred.'

'How many witnesses have you heard so far?'

'None fully. The plaintiff was in the box for three or four weeks and then the defendant interposed to ask if a witness who was going abroad could be called. The plaintiff agreed. No sooner is that witness out of the box – well, perhaps, "sooner" isn't quite the right word – he was in the box for three weeks – when the plaintiff's counsel asks if he can interpose a witness on somewhat similar grounds. Of course the defendant agreed. And that's how it's been going on all the time.'

Six months later the case was still going on merrily and it started to become one of the sights to which guides in London took foreign visitors. After a year well-to-do lawyers from America flew over to have a look, while after two years the case had become a kind of national institution. Subject only to the rules of contempt of Court, it was a safe subject for comedians and after-dinner speakers until it became too stale even for them.

One of the people who came to visit the Court from time to time and who appeared to take an almost paternal interest in it was a multi-millionaire named Rufus Catchpole. He never spoke to anyone connected with the case but from time to time met eminent visitors like himself and chatted to them in the corridor.

'They're on the libel today, I see. I wonder when they'll reach the false imprisonment,' he said to an acquaintance one day.

'I didn't know that came into it.'

'It didn't at first, but I happened to be here some months ago when the defendant asked for leave to add it to his counterclaim.'

'Didn't the other side object?'

'Oh – no. They welcomed the opportunity of dealing with it.'

'What about the judge? I should have thought he'd have had enough by now.'

'Well – he didn't really see what he could do about it. You see, if he'd refused to allow the amendment, the defendant could have issued a writ and, before this case was over, the new one would have been ready for trial, and it wouldn't have been right to make the parties have another judge for that one case.'

'Didn't you have a case before old Broadbent once?'

'Yes,' said the multi-millionaire, 'I did.' And then he changed the subject. They went into Court to hear the judge start to deal with a claim that Mr Anstruther's fence was 13/4" much to the right – as you looked at it from the road.

The case which Rufus Catchpole had had before Mr Justice Broadbent had not been of much importance in itself; but it was of importance to Mr Catchpole. The judge decided against him on an issue of fact on which it was hopeless to appeal. Mr Catchpole did not ordinarily indulge in litigation, although his means were such that he could have done so with impunity. That is to say, with impunity as far as money was concerned, but not as far as pride was concerned. He considered that Mr Justice Broadbent had tried the case outrageously and that he had not simply come to a wrong conclusion but that he had shown himself, in Mr Catchpole's view, wholly unfitted to be a judge.

After he had consulted his counsel on the subject of appeal and been satisfied that it was hopeless, Mr Catchpole began to consider how he could protect the public from Mr Justice Broadbent.

'He ought never to be allowed to try another case,' he said to himself. 'How can I prevent him?'

Mr Catchpole knew that it would be quite useless to make any complaint against the judge. He knew that he could only be removed from office if both Houses of Parliament asked the Queen for his removal. Such a thing had never occurred in living memory and, even if it had, he knew that there was nothing he could urge which would persuade a single Member of Parliament to take up the cudgels on his behalf. The judge had rejected his evidence and accepted that of his opponent. Only he, Rufus Catchpole, and his opponent knew how wrong the judge had been.

But, in his view, a judge who could make such a mistake ought not to be allowed to try cases. He had approached a consideration of the evidence in a way which showed, in Mr Catchpole's view, that the judge simply did not understand how to recognise the truth. Yet he knew that any disappointed litigant might say the same and that, unless he himself could do something, no one else would. He had no particular grudge against Mr Justice Broadbent. He simply wanted to prevent him from perpetrating further injustices. Unless he did something, the judge would go on doing so for another three years.

He finally hit on the plan which resulted in the litigation between Mr Tiptree and Mr Anstruther. Completely unknown to their counsel and solicitors these two gentlemen, at the request and expense of Mr Catchpole, were waging an imaginary war, the object of which was to keep Mr Justice Broadbent out of judicial circulation until the date for his retirement arrived. The lawyers had not the least suspicion of what was really happening and so they carried out their clients' requirements with skill and assiduity and to their great personal enrichment. Their clients said that they appreciated that the time the case was taking might interfere with their counsel's other work and they were accordingly not only most accommodating about fees but agreed to employ several additional counsel so as to enable the protagonists to give some time to the rest of their practice.

Towards the end of the three years left of Mr Justice Broadbent's judicial life he began to warn the parties of the gravity of the situation. 'It will be a little unfortunate,' he said, 'if at the end of three years the case has to start again before another judge.'

Counsel respectfully agreed that it would indeed be a little unfortunate and added that they would each of them do all they could to ensure that this unhappy event did not take place.

Mr Catchpole, however, was determined that the judge should not try one other case and rather than risk the disputes between Mr Anstruther and Mr Tiptree coming to an untimely end two days before the judge's birthday, he continued to prime his nominees with sufficient additional material, including documents and witnesses and even points of law, which ensured that the judge would indeed have the case on his hands right up to the date of his compulsory retirement.

On the date before he automatically retired the case was far from ended and counsel and the judge were behaving rather like cricketers continuing in a match which was bound to be drawn. Apart from occasional sixes (such as: 'Remind me of what you said about that on the first day of this case, Mr Boles'), the players continued in a desultory manner, all of them being quite assured that they were achieving nothing. Even had Mr Boles reduced one of his opponent's chief witnesses to a stuttering withdrawal of all he had so far said, it would have made no difference. At 4.15 p.m. Mr Justice Broadbent would rise and the case would have to start all over again before another judge. Apart from the fact that they were being paid, all those concerned might have been better employed in reading the newspapers.

But at 4 p.m. precisely Mr Anstruther got up and left the Court. At 4.1 p.m. Mr Tiptree followed his example. At 4.10 p.m. they returned to Court and spoke to their respective solicitors. At 4.13 p.m. counsel on each side asked if his Lordship would give them a moment. And at 4.15 p.m. Mr Boles announced that he was happy to say that his Lordship would no longer be troubled with the case, as the parties had happily come to terms. These were that all the claims would be withdrawn and each side would pay its own costs. Counsel thanked the judge most sincerely for the care he had given to the case and said that their respective clients were most grateful. They wished his Lordship a happy retirement.

The judge rose and was soon on his way home. He lived a little way out in the country and went by train. Mr Catchpole was well aware of this and could not resist travelling in the same carriage. The judge did not remember his face and they sat in silence for some time. Eventually Mr Catchpole spoke:

'Forgive me mentioning it, Sir Charles,' he said, 'but I've followed your case with interest. Are you relieved that it's over?'

'I expect the parties are,' said the judge. 'It must have cost them I don't know how much.'

Mr Catchpole did not say that he did know how much. He could afford it, though it was indeed a very large amount. But he did not grudge it. He had achieved his object. Not another case had that judge tried from the time he started Tiptree against Anstruther.

'You must have found it rather wearing,' said Mr Catchpole.

'Well,' said the judge, 'it was not uninteresting in parts. But I must admit that as a whole it was rather a bore. If I'd known how long it was going to last, I'd have refused to take it. They said it was a long case, but naturally I thought of a week or a couple of weeks at the most. Very few cases take longer than that.'

'Well, at least I'm glad it interested you in parts.'

'That hardly made up for the time it took. You see, if it hadn't been for that case, I should have retired three years ago. But, as I said, I suppose it's been worse for the parties than for me. The expense, I mean.'

The Wanted Man

'My father assured me,' said Mr Partridge, 'that there never had been and never would be a port year like 1912. " '96, '04 and '08 were very good," he used to say, "very good indeed, but we had to wait until 1912 for perfection." All I say is that I wish he could have lived until 1927. That would have made him think.'

He looked happily at his guests.

'It's still pretty good, isn't it?' he asked. It was not just politeness that made them agree. There were grunts of approval all round the table. After all, they had had a superb dinner, not the first at Mr Partridge's house by any means, and, although 1927 is a long way off, the port had stood the journey remarkably well.

Mr Partridge had been in the neighbourhood about a couple of years at this time and it had not been long after his arrival that people began to notice him. Not indeed because he pressed himself upon them, for he did nothing of the kind. But because he appeared to be a man with most of the virtues required of a good neighbour. He was friendly but not too friendly, modest, generous and with a dry sense of humour. And he could talk. The subjects in which he appeared most interested were wine and crime. He found ready listeners for both of them, particularly as he usually provided excellent examples of the former before discussing the latter.

A close observer would have realised that Mr Partridge had come to the locality with the deliberate intention of becoming part of it. But he did not try to force the pace. That would have been fatal. A stranger has to play himself in. It is not sufficient to give generously to Church and other local funds or to drive your car with due consideration for others using the road, or to respond with a cheerful 'good day' whenever greeted. There is no welcome for newcomers who pounce on old-established residents.

Mr Partridge did not pounce. He simply took advantage of every opportunity of being of some use, however slight, to anyone who came his way. It was not, therefore, surprising that the Vicar began to sing his praises. This was not because he was known to put £5 in the plate every Sunday. On the contrary, anxious as the Vicar was to obtain funds, he mistrusted strangers who put in too much. Indeed, on one occasion he had had a great struggle with his conscience when a notorious bookmaker, who had been convicted of receiving stolen goods, put £100 in the plate on Easter Sunday. It was a difficult point. Theoretically no one knew who had put it in. But twenty five-pound notes cannot be smuggled into the bag like a threepenny piece. The sidesman told the Vicar, and the Vicar wondered what he ought to do. He wondered still more when the donor was arrested and charged with complicity in a bank robbery. But, although by this time the money had been spent, he did not hesitate. He told the Chief Constable. And the Chief Constable said 'Like some of your colleagues – if you'll forgive my saying so, Vicar – you talk too much.'

'But I couldn't be a party to ...' began the Vicar.

'And d'you think,' cut in the Chief Constable, 'that I would be a party either? If these notes could be traced, I should be the first to say that we must try to trace them.

But they can't be. I'm sorry, Vicar, but there it is. You must put up with your misfortunes. Banks used to keep a note of the numbers of five-pound notes, but they don't any longer. I apologise on their behalf. Shall we go in to tea?'

It will be understood, therefore, that the Vicar was a little touchy about large gifts on Sunday. So, at the very first, he viewed Mr Partridge with suspicion. But it did not last long. Mr Partridge did not look or talk or behave like a bookmaker or a robber of banks. He had a large moustache and a beard to match. And whoever heard of a bookmaker with a beard? Of course he might have grown them as a disguise, but such an unworthy thought never crossed the Vicar's mind. Not to begin with, at any rate.

After he had served his six months' period of probation, Mr Partridge began to be generally accepted. And within a year he was on visiting terms with everyone. He had bought a small house with a little land and he had made the house very comfortable. He was a bachelor or a widower – he never made it quite clear which – and he was looked after by a housekeeper whom he brought with him. She was of obvious respectability and, even more important, she was a first-class cook. Local labour supplied his other needs.

But, popular as he became, Mr Partridge was always something of a mystery. Most people have a job or have retired from one. No one could ever find out exactly what Mr Partridge's position was, except that he was obviously very comfortably off. Perhaps he had been a successful retail tradesman – even possibly a wine merchant – and was shy of mentioning it. Time and again attempts had been made to find out what he was or had been. At first attempts were indirect, then direct and then indirect again.

'And what do you do – retired, I suppose?'

'Eh?' said Mr Partridge, pleasantly enough. 'Have some more port.'

It became a sort of game trying to find out what Mr Partridge did. Once the wife of the Chief Constable asked him point-blank. 'Mr Partridge – you must tell us what you do or what you used to do?' she said playfully.

'Why should I?' said Mr Partridge equally playfully. 'How charming that dress is.'

They gave it up in the end and accepted him for what he was, a cheerful friend and a good neighbour.

On the occasion with which this story started, they continued to discuss the wine for a short time, and then turned happily to crime.

'They've never got that fellow who escaped two years ago,' said the Colonel. 'Wonder what he's doing. Out of the country, I expect.'

'It's not me,' said Mr Partridge, and they all laughed. But, later that evening after they had left Mr Partridge, some of his guests began to examine the possibility more closely. At first jokingly, but later more seriously. After all, they knew nothing about him. Where had he come from? Why was he so reticent about his past? It was certainly very odd. They consulted the Chief Constable.

'Are you being funny?' he asked.

'Well, the man must be somewhere,' said the Colonel. 'And where did Partridge come from? He never tells us. What did he do? No one knows.'

'Well – what d'you expect me to do? Take his fingerprints?'

'Why not?' said the Colonel.

'Really!' said the Chief Constable. 'You go and dine with a man and eat his food, drink his wine, and then take his fingerprints. Well – you'll have to do it – not me.'

'I didn't mean openly,' said the Colonel. 'We can give him a sticky plate to catch hold of or something.'

'That's even worse,' said the Chief Constable. 'Is that what they taught you in the Army? People complain at police methods – but I prefer ours to those. No – if I had the slightest suspicion I'd go straight to him and ask him point-blank. That's the only decent thing to do. Isn't it, Vicar?'

The Vicar thought for a moment. 'You're obviously right,' he said. 'It's the only way it could be done.'

'And I may add,' said the Chief Constable, 'I'd want a bit more evidence than we have at present before I did anything. Just because a chap doesn't want to talk about his past. Whose business is his past, anyway? Why should he tell us?'

The conversation ended and things went on in the district much as they had before. Mr Partridge was as pleasant and generous as ever and was welcomed wherever he went. But every time the newspapers, for want of news, referred to the fact that the escaped prisoner had now been missing for so much longer, one or two people started to talk again and there were some uncomfortable moments. Particularly, if Mr Partridge happened to come in, just after they had been discussing the matter.

But one day, to the pleasure of all of them, the matter was cleared up. The chief protagonists in the suspicion game were all sitting together talking about something else. The wireless was on. It was the news.

'This afternoon George Brown – the prisoner who escaped nearly three years ago – was arrested in London.'

It was the best news they had heard for a long time. They all liked Mr Partridge, even those who had their suspicions, and it was a great relief to find it was all a myth.

'It just shows how unfair people are,' said one of them, looking at the Colonel.

'You're quite right, old boy,' said the Colonel. 'You mean me, and I agree with you. I'm damned sorry.' He paused a moment. 'Look, I tell you what,' he said; 'I'm going straight over to confess and apologise to him. And I'll present him with my last two bottles of Romanee-Conti. That'll show I mean it.'

The others agreed and each decided to give a similar token of his contrition. In consequence the estate car which shortly afterwards drew up at Mr Partridge's house looked inside like a wine merchant's delivery van. One of the offerings was champagne, and it was confidently expected that Mr Partridge would open a bottle or two to celebrate the occasion. They were sure that of all men he would be generous in accepting their apologies.

But they were disappointed.

'I'm afraid it must have been a great shock to you,' said the detective-inspector who let them in. 'D'you think I could have your statements now?'

Mock Trial

'Personally,' said the American lawyer, 'I think mock trials are a waste of time. You can never get the atmosphere of the real trial into them. So they either degenerate into a farce, with counsel asking silly questions and the witnesses giving sillier answers, or they are plain straight boring. There's nothing more dramatic than a real trial, and the reason it's dramatic is because everyone knows how much depends on the result. Once you know it isn't real, the whole essence of the thing has gone. Moots are quite a different matter: proper legal arguments on questions of law for the benefit of young lawyers are excellent, but mock trials – ', he waved his hand in a deprecating gesture, ' – I prefer television.'

'Well,' said the police commander, 'I once took a small part in a mock trial which was fought in deadly earnest, and a great deal depended on the result.'

'A bet or something?'

'A mere matter of life or death,' said the commander.

'Depended on the result of a mock trial?' said the American, increduously. 'Sure you're not allowing yourself a little dramatic licence?'

'None whatever. Your money back, if you don't agree when I've told you.'

'I suppose it's an escape story or something like that – a sort of legal Wooden Horse.'

'Not at all. It was at the Old Bailey.'

'A mock trial at the Old Bailey? They wouldn't allow that sort of thing in the States. Bring the law into contempt.'

'Well this might have, but it didn't. I'm surprised you haven't read about it.'

'Maybe I have – but I don't recognise it yet. Fire ahead, and I'll stop you if I know about it.'

'Does the Candy case mean nothing to you?'

'Candy? Not a thing.'

'George Candy – he was tried for murder at the Old Bailey about twenty-five years ago.'

'I was only ten then. So it looks as though you've a clear run.'

'It was not a very sensational case in the first instance, except that every murder case is to some extent sensational, particularly if the prisoner pleads "Not Guilty" and means it. The evidence was in quite a small compass too. It was all over in one day, bar the summing-up and the verdict. I was an ordinary detective-constable at the time.'

'A witness?'

'Not in the normal sense of the word. I never went into the witness-box. But I witnessed something all right.'

'Go ahead. I won't interrupt any more. It sounds intriguing.'

'It was. Except for the summing-up, the case was finished on a Friday and it wasn't more than second page news on the Saturday morning. But on Saturday night things began to happen. I didn't know about them at the time, but it all came out later. All I knew at first was that on Monday the trial was adjourned until the next day. Nothing very extraordinary in that. I forget what explanation was given – something quite normal. The public thought nothing of it. As I've said, they didn't think much of the trial anyway, except that it was a case of murder. On the Tuesday the judge summed up. I remember pretty well what he said. Among other things, he said something like this: "Members of the jury, suspicion is not enough, even grave suspicion. You have to be satisfied beyond all reasonable doubt that the prisoner committed this crime. Can you be so satisfied on the evidence, members of the jury? And let me remind you once again that you are trying this man on the evidence which has been called before you. Not upon what you have read in the newspapers before the prisoner was arrested – not on gossip or tittle-tattle you may have heard, but on the evidence you heard coming from that witness-box and upon nothing else. English law so recoils from the possibility of an innocent man being convicted that it is one of our maxims that it is better that a hundred guilty men should be acquitted than that one innocent man should be condemned."

'He said a good deal more in much the same strain – in other words, he summed up for an acquittal, and without retiring we brought in a verdict of Not Guilty.'

'You? I thought you were a detective then. I didn't know the police served on juries.'

'Well, I served on that one. But I haven't told you what happened during the trial. The judge, who was trying the case, lived a little way out of London. He had a wife and a small daughter. He'd lost his first wife and married again. Hence the small girl. On the Saturday night two masked men raided the judge's house, kidnapped the small girl at pistol point, and warned the judge that, unless he obtained an acquittal of the man who was being tried before him, he would never see his daughter again. Then they left hurriedly with the little girl and without leaving an address or anything which might enable them to be identified. They were quite polite but very, very firm. As soon as the prisoner was acquitted, the little girl would be returned safe and sound. But if he were convicted, the little girl would be disposed of. The judge, of course, immediately spoke to the police, but it was a very delicate situation. I've no doubt he discussed the matter with a lot of legal high-ups – the Lord Chancellor, the Lord Chief Justice, and so on. But, of course, I didn't know anything of that at the time. They didn't confide in me. But, when we gave our verdict, the prisoner was set free and his friends kept their promise and the little girl was returned safe and sound.'

'I can't believe,' interrupted the American, 'that even to save his own daughter, an English judge would give a false summing-up.'

'Well, I heard it,' said the commander, 'and I can assure you we had no option but to say "Not Guilty".'

'But a jury doesn't *have* to do what the judge suggests, however strongly he suggests it.'

'I know,' said the commander, 'that was the trouble.'

'Trouble?' queried the American. 'I thought you did what the judge wanted.'

'We certainly did,' said the commander, 'but I thought you said you wouldn't interrupt.'

'Sorry, I won't, but I just don't know where I am.'

'Well, see if this throws any light on the situation. As soon as the little girl was returned, the prisoner was rearrested.'

'I'm sorry,' said the American, 'but I must come in again. What about your doctrine of *autrefois acquit*? You can't try a man twice for the same crime. He'd been acquitted. That was an end of it. Or has your law been altered?'

'No,' said the commander, 'we haven't altered that law yet. As a matter of fact, I was one of those who arrested him.'

'You? But you were on the jury. Sorry – there I go again. Fire ahead. I'll put a handkerchief in my mouth.'

'I went with an inspector and a sergeant. I'd been shadowing Candy ever since he'd been let out. When we picked him up, he took much the same view as you did. "What's all this?" he said. "I've been acquitted. You can't take me again for that. What's the charge? You've no evidence that I – " He paused long enough for the inspector to put in "That you what?" "That I had anything to do with – " Another pause. "Yes," put in the inspector again, "with what?" But Candy had pulled himself together by then. "With anything," he said. "I thought you might be referring to a little matter of kidnapping," said the inspector. "Never heard of it," said Candy. "Funny," said the inspector, "we thought you might have." "Well, I haven't," said Candy, "So I'll trouble you to let me go. It's a free country and I've been acquitted. So, good afternoon." But they didn't let him go.

' "You're under arrest," said the inspector.

' "What for?" said Candy.

' "You'll see."

' "I've a right to know now."

' "Oh, no you haven't," said the inspector. "Are you coming quietly or shall we put the handcuffs on?"

' "Well – you'll have to tell me at the police station," said Candy.

' "We aren't going to a police station," said the inspector.

' "What *is* this?" said Candy. "If you arrest me, you've got to charge me. I know my rights."

' "Not all of them," said the inspector. "Come on now."

' "Where are we going?"

' "To the Old Bailey."

' "You can't do that. I've got to be charged before a magistrate first."

' "You have been."

' "What are you talking about?" said Candy. "I haven't been near any magistrate since I went for trial on the murder charge."

' "Quite right," said the inspector. "That's what you're going to the Old Bailey for – murder."

' "But you can't do that," said Candy. "You know perfectly well I've been acquitted."

' "That's just what you haven't been," said the inspector. Candy laughed.

' "Have you gone mad?" he said. "I happened to be there," he said sarcastically. "I was in the dock. The clerk asked the foreman of the jury if they were all agreed that I was Not Guilty, he said they were and I was let out. If that didn't happen, you can certify me straight away. If that didn't happen, I'm not here now, and it's all a horrible dream."

' "Well, it's not a dream," said the inspector, "and what you say is quite right up to a point."

' "Then stop this nonsense, and let me go," said Candy.

' "I said it was right up to a point," said the inspector. "It was right up to the point where you were in the dock. You were in the dock all right and that's where you're going now – back in the dock."

' "But the jury said 'Not Guilty'."

' "The jury didn't," said the inspector.

' "There's nothing wrong with my hearing," said Candy, "and, even if there were, everyone else heard the same and they let me go. P'raps you're going to tell me they found me guilty. Maybe you'll add that I was sentenced to death and have already been hanged."

' "No," said the inspector. "You haven't been hanged – yet. As a matter of fact, the jury hasn't given a verdict at all yet. That's what you're going back for. That – and the summing-up first, of course."

' "If this is a game," said Candy, "it's not a funny one. The judge summed up. I heard him. Don't take my word for it. Ask him. He summed up all right."

' "I suppose he did in a way," said the inspector, "but the jury didn't hear it."

' "If they were asleep or deaf, is that my fault?" said Candy. "Anyway they said 'Not Guilty', which is all that matters to me."

' "I tell you," said the inspector, "the jury didn't say anything at all."

' "Well, the foreman then," said Candy. "They don't all speak, you know. I'd have thought you might have known that by this time. The foreman speaks for them. And when he's said 'Guilty' or 'Not Guilty', the clerk asks him if that is the verdict of them all, and he says 'Yes' – and that's what happened in this case – only he said 'Not Guilty'."

' "The foreman of the jury," said the inspector, "couldn't very well have said 'Not Guilty', as he wasn't at the Old Bailey."

' "I suppose you'll tell me I wasn't there either," said Candy.

' "Oh – yes – you were there – and the judge – and counsel – but the jury weren't. They had a holiday."

' "Then perhaps you'd tell me who were sitting in the jury box. Or perhaps you'll say it was empty."

' "No, it wasn't empty."

' "Then who was in it if it wasn't the jury?"

' "Twelve policemen, as a matter of fact, or, to be accurate, eleven policemen and one policewoman. In plain clothes, of course."

' "Really!" sneered Candy. "I should have thought they would have been better employed stopping the slaughter on the roads."

' "Well," said the inspector, "they were employed in stopping slaughter – the slaughter of one little girl – whose death had been promised by friends of yours if you were convicted. So they arranged a mock trial for you, Candy, and you're going back to get on with the real one now."

' "But – but," spluttered Candy, "they can't do a thing like that."

' "They've done it," said the inspector. "And between you and me, it was a pretty smart idea. I don't know who thought of it."

' "It's an outrage."

' "And how would you describe the murder of a little girl?" asked the inspector. "No, Mr Candy," he went on, "we've no evidence at present that you had anything to do with the kidnapping yourself, but, if friends of yours do that kind of thing for your benefit, you must address your complaints to them if the plan doesn't work."

' "But the jury looked the same," said Candy.

' "Thank you," said the inspector. "That's a compliment and we didn't have much time. They wore the same clothes as the real jury, who were taken into the secret and lent them. I did my best to choose people who looked sufficiently like the people you'd seen. And I'm much obliged to you for saying you didn't notice any difference. Here's one of them, as a matter of fact. Second row at the extreme left he sat", and the inspector pointed to me. I was in uniform. "But, of course, as I've told you, he wasn't dressed like this, and I don't suppose you ever gave him more than a casual glance."

' "Well – if twelve people in that box say 'Not Guilty' and I'm let out of the dock – I say I'm acquitted."

' "I dare say you do," said the inspector. "But you're no more acquitted than if twelve of your friends in a public house said so. Or twelve people up in the gallery. The only people who can say 'Not Guilty' – or 'Guilty' for that matter – are the twelve people on the jury who were sworn to try the case and who heard the evidence. They had a day off when you were let out."

' "I shall see my lawyers about this."

' "Of course you will," said the inspector. "We've told them to meet you at the Old Bailey. But you don't imagine we've done this without advice. If your lawyers differ from the Attorney-General on this point, I'll be very much surprised – and they'll be wrong, if that's of any interest to you."

'Well, Candy fumed and swore and talked of all the things he was going to do. But there was nothing in fact which he could do about it. Of course it all came out in the Press and created a tremendous sensation. But no one criticised the authorities for doing what they'd done. And I've often tried to think what else they could have done which would have got the little girl back and at the same time ensured that Candy was properly tried. Can you think of anything else?'

'I take it I may speak now,' said the American. 'No, I can't say that I can, and I hand it to the chap who thought of it. But what happened in the end?'

'Well, that had its funny side. D'you remember saying that a jury isn't bound to follow a judge's suggestions and I said that that was the trouble?'

'Yes.'

'Well – we, of course, weren't a jury at all. We were just a lot of actors and only one of us had a speaking part – the chap who played the foreman. But if we'd been a real jury – you couldn't have been absolutely certain that we'd have found the prisoner Not Guilty even with that summing-up.'

'I dare say, but I don't see what that's got to do with it.'

'Well, you will. You see, the odd thing was that when the judge came to sum up – properly, I mean, with a new jury – he said almost identically what he'd said to us, and the chap got off again. You see, the evidence wasn't very strong anyway – but I think they were quite right not to take a chance, don't you?'

The Wife in the Train

The young woman came into Court 1 at the Old Bailey as unobtrusively as was possible for anyone as attractive as she was. The man in the dock turned his head and saw her. After a pause he gave a slight smile which she returned almost shyly. Then they both devoted their full attention to the proceedings.

The foreman was about to give the jury's verdict. Even in a non-capital case it is a tense moment. So much depends on the foreman's words. At the most the total will be six words, at the least three. But the difference to the person in the dock cannot be measured. He and his friends and relatives find the suspense greatest while the jury is filing back into its place. Counsel for the prosecution usually has no burning desire to secure a conviction but he will in most cases be more satisfied if there is one. Usually the suspense in his case is more because of the human drama which is being played in front of him than because of the effect on his own career. Counsel for the defence, on the other hand, has a much greater interest in the matter; old or young, experienced or otherwise, believing in his client's guilt or suspecting that he might actually be innocent, he wants to hear 'Not Guilty'. No doubt at all about that. They will be sweet words for him. Not, of course, as sweet as for the prisoner but very sweet indeed. And, if he is young and ambitious and perhaps just starting to make his way up the shaky ladder of the law, it will seem terribly important.

The judge, Mr Justice Brace, on the other hand, did not mind in the least what the verdict was. He was perfectly satisfied of the accused's guilt, but he had summed up fairly and he would not mind if the jury chose to acquit. That was their province. He was not a judge who summed up one way or the other. He felt impartial and did his best to appear so. He was a man of sixty and had been a judge now for ten years. He was the right type for a judge, a man of decision, ability and integrity. He had, of course, his faults. For example, he had a tendency to impatience with lawyers slower-witted than himself. This particularly showed itself in his treatment of younger members of the Bar. He expected them to know their briefs and their law as well as older men. And, of course, most of them did not. In consequence, young men found him awe-inspiring, and sometimes literally shook with fear when they were in front of him.

He was, with one qualification, a fair and kindly man but his worst fault was that he did not like to be corrected. He was usually in the right but he recognised that he, like anyone else, could make mistakes. He was ready enough to say so when he saw that he was mistaken but he liked to find it out for himself or at least to be the first to announce it. He did not like other people to do so. Naturally this was inevitable from time to time but it had to be done very diplomatically. When so done, he would swiftly appear to have realised the mistake himself and would frankly acknowledge it. Experienced counsel knew his weakness and how to deal with it and would never say: 'With respect, your Lordship is wrong and I will make this assertion good.'

Instead they would gently insinuate the point into the judge's mind and, as often as not, he would be the first to say that he was wrong. As he was usually right and young men usually wrong it was not often that they had the opportunity of having to correct him with justification. When they themselves were mistaken and had not been diplomatic in their method of trying to show that it was the judge who was mistaken, he made them feel very small indeed. He used few words but they were very biting and no one ever forgot them. In the odd case when he was himself wrong and the young barrister pointed out the error tactlessly, he would of course be forced to admit the mistake but he usually did so in a way calculated to give the young man at least some discomfort and sometimes a good deal of it. It was odd that an otherwise fair-minded man should suffer from this defect. No doubt it flowed from conceit, which is an inevitable occupational disease of the Bar as a whole.

'Members of the Jury, are you agreed upon your verdict?'

'We are.'

'Do you find the accused, Daniel Moore, guilty or not guilty?'

'Guilty.'

'Guilty, and that is the verdict of you all?'

'It is.'

The man in the dock turned his head and gave a rueful smile at the young woman, but she was not looking in his direction.

Roger Newbury, counsel for the prosecution, then called the police officer in charge of the case who stated that the accused was aged 30 and had never been in trouble before. He had had a good education and had been working in the City at the time of the offence, one of obtaining money by false pretences. It was then stated that the accused admitted three other offences similar in nature to the one of which he had been convicted and wished them to be taken into consideration. The officer added that the accused was a married man with no children.

'Mr Blaize,' said the judge eventually, 'do you wish to say anything in mitigation?'

Arnold Blaize got up.

'If your Lordship pleases,' he said.

He was an able young man and, apart from one unfortunate episode, had managed to get on pretty well with the judge before whom it was his first appearance. He had, however, been rapped over the knuckles pretty smartly once for suggesting that the judge had made a mistake in his understanding of the answer of a witness, when in fact he had not done so. As Blaize had done this in the middle of the summing-up, when no judge welcomes an interruption, the reproof which the young man received was delivered in carefully chosen words, which would have made some young barristers wish to retire from the Bar forthwith. However, Arnold Blaize was not so easily dismayed and he was determined to say all that could be said for his client. The young woman and the prisoner looked anxiously at him as he began his address.

'My Lord,' he said, 'my client wishes to express to your Lordship his deep regret for these offences.'

'He's sorry, is he?' said the judge.

'Very, my Lord.'

'I should have been more ready to take notice of that,' said the judge, 'if he had pleaded guilty. He pleaded not guilty, he said he was not guilty and now he has been found guilty he says he's sorry. I'm sure he is sorry – that he's been found out.'

'My Lord,' persisted Blaize, 'my client says that, if your Lordship will take a lenient view, he will never trouble your Lordship again.'

'He hasn't troubled *me*. It's the public he's troubled. I can't possibly overlook this.'

'Oh, my Lord,' said Blaize, 'I wasn't suggesting your Lordship should overlook it. But my client is a young married man with an excellent character hitherto and I would respectfully suggest that a fine might meet the case.'

'Because your client has means,' said the judge, 'he needn't think he can buy himself out of this. A poor man couldn't pay a fine.'

'But with respect, my Lord, you shouldn't send my client to prison because he has means.'

'I shall send him to prison because of his crimes, not because of his means.'

'But your Lordship implied that, because a poor man would have to go to prison in default of payment of a fine, your Lordship was going to send my client to prison.'

'I implied nothing of the kind,' said the judge.

'Then with respect, my Lord, I don't follow your Lordship's reference to a poor man. A poor man has nothing to do with it if, poor or rich, he should be sent to prison.'

This was a good point and the judge knew it. He found silence the easiest answer to it. Silence is one of the stronger judicial weapons. Blaize waited for him to say something but he remained silent.

'Go on, please, Mr Blaize,' he said eventually.

'Would your Lordship be good enough to tell me what your Lordship's reference to a poor man meant? Then perhaps I can deal with the point which is in your Lordship's mind.'

'I am not here to answer your questions, Mr Blaize,' said the judge.

'Of course not,' said Blaize, 'but I'm sure your Lordship wants to do justice and, if a prisoner's counsel can't understand an observation of the judge, I am sure you would wish to make it plain to him.'

Again he waited for a word from the Bench but there was none.

'No doubt it's entirely my fault,' Blaize went on, 'but it is my client who will suffer.'

'He should have thought of that before he started on this criminal enterprise.'

At this stage the young woman and the prisoner, who had been looking intently at Blaize, looked for a moment at each other. 'It's hopeless,' their faces said.

'My Lord,' Blaize went on, 'I was submitting to your Lordship that this offence could be met with a fine and your Lordship said that a poor man couldn't pay a fine.'

'You said that before,' said the judge.

'I respectfully submit that your Lordship should not send my client to prison because *he could* pay a fine.'

'It is not in my opinion a case for a fine,' said the judge.

'Then, my Lord,' said Blaize, 'with the greatest possible respect I do not follow your Lordship's reference to a poor man being unable to pay a fine.'

'That's the third time you've said that,' said the judge.

'And with respect,' said Blaize boldly, 'it's the third time your Lordship has failed to deal with the point.'

'Behave yourself, Mr Blaize,' said the judge, using the word most calculated to make a witness or an advocate feel that he is back at school.

'I intend no discourtesy to your Lordship,' said Blaize.

'Well, you show it,' said the judge.

'I'm sorry, my Lord.'

'So is your client,' said the judge, 'and for much the same reason.'

'My Lord,' said Blaize, 'it's my duty to say all that can be said on behalf of my client.'

'It is also your duty to behave yourself, and mine to see that you do.'

'It is also my duty to see that I understand your Lordship's observations and your Lordship was comparing my client with a poor man, saying – '

'Leave the poor man out of it, Mr Blaize,' said the judge. 'I'm dealing with your client who is not a poor man. I simply said that, because a man has money, that doesn't mean he can avoid punishment for his crimes.'

'But, my Lord,' said Blaize, 'if the crime deserves imprisonment, a poor man would have to go to prison just as much as a rich man. Your Lordship said a poor man couldn't pay a fine. And, unless that meant that my client had to go to prison because *he could* pay a fine, I don't know what it meant and I respectfully ask your Lordship for guidance on the matter.'

'I have already asked you to leave the poor man out of it. Is there anything else you wish to say?'

Another hopeless look passed between the prisoner and the young woman.

'Your Lordship must have considered the possibility of a fine in this case,' Blaize went on.

'I've done nothing of the kind,' said the judge. 'I tell you it's not a case for a fine.'

'Then, my Lord,' said Blaize, 'I still don't see where the poor man comes in.'

'Sit down, please, Mr Blaize,' said the judge.

'But, my Lord ...'

'Sit down, please. When you repeat yourself a fourth time I'm entitled to assume that you have nothing further to say. Sit down. Thank you.'

Blaize sat down. The prisoner looked resigned. A look of wild fury was on the young woman.

'Daniel Moore,' said the judge, addressing the prisoner, 'you have been convicted of or admitted a number of frauds and, although you have hitherto borne a good character, I cannot possibly give effect to your learned counsel's submission. You will go to prison for twelve months.'

'You beast,' hissed the young woman but not loud enough to be heard by any official.

Six weeks later Mr Justice Brace got into the carriage of a non-corridor train at a London terminus. The carriage was empty and he lit a cigarette and started to read the paper. Just before the train left, the young woman, who had been at the trial at the Old Bailey, got in and sat down. She sat on the opposite side of the carriage to the judge in the farther corner. After the train had been going a minute or two she suddenly spoke rather falteringly.

'My Lord ...' she began.

The judge looked at her. He saw a very attractive young woman whom he did not know. He could not possibly have forgotten her, if he had ever met her. But she looked respectable.

'Yes, madam?' he said, 'I don't think I've had the pleasure ...'

'No, my Lord.' There was silence for a few seconds and then the girl began again.

'My Lord ...'

The use of the expression 'My Lord' rather irritated the judge. He was not going to get involved in conversation but at least he could put that right.

'Forgive me, madam,' he said, 'but you don't call judges "my Lord" out of Court.'

'What should I call you then? "Sir" doesn't sound right.'

'Well, madam, quite frankly, as we don't know one another, there appears to be no need to call me anything.'

The judge retired into his paper. But he didn't read it. He was a little unhappy about his curtness. After all, she hadn't been impertinent or offensive in any way. He oughtn't to have treated her like that.

'Please don't think I wish to be offensive, madam,' he said, 'but I like to read when travelling.'

'I might have been a friend of a relative of yours,' said the girl.

'Then you wouldn't have called me "my Lord." '

'I might have been an uneducated friend of a relative.'

'Are you, madam? A friend of a relative, I mean.'

'No. But I still don't know what to call you.'

'There's no need to call me anything, madam. If you would like the window open or shut or you want a match, please ask.'

'It's a non-smoker as a matter of fact.'

'Oh,' said the judge. 'Oh – I'm sorry. I apologise, madam. I'll put it out.'

'It wasn't that. I'd love a cigarette myself.'

The judge offered her one of his but she refused, saying that she only smoked her own.

The judge went back to his paper. Occasionally he glanced up at her but immediately went back to the paper when he caught her eye. He was a little intrigued to know why she had started the conversation. What had she wanted?

'How should I attract your attention,' she said eventually, 'without calling you something?'

'Well, you have, madam. Did you want to ask me something?'

'Not ask, really. Tell.'

The judge was not quite sure now what to do. He was slightly intrigued but he certainly had no intention of picking up a strange young woman, however attractive, in a railway carriage. At the same time, she was well spoken and he supposed it couldn't do any harm just to be polite.

'You want to tell me something?' he asked.

'Yes. May I?'

This was an awkward question. To say no would have been rude, to say yes would be to encourage conversation. For the moment he tried silence.

'May I?' she repeated.

There was nothing else for it.

'Certainly, madam.'

'Oh, thank you. I didn't expect it to be so easy. That's my second piece of luck. The guard forgot to lock you in.'

'How do you know that?'

'I've followed you here for the last six weeks.' That made things quite certain.

'I'm afraid I don't wish to continue this conversation, madam,' he said. He retired very deliberately into the paper.

'But you said I could tell you something,' said the girl. 'And I'm going to. You can pretend not to listen if you like, but you can't help hearing. I said I'd been following you here for the last six weeks, don't you want to know why? Don't you?'

'No, madam,' said the judge.

'Then I'll tell you. I've been following you here ever since you gave Daniel Moore twelve months at the Old

Bailey six weeks ago. It was a disgraceful exhibition. You wouldn't even listen to his counsel.'

The judge thought for a moment or two. Then: 'You're the wife, I suppose?' he asked.

'Yes, but how did you know?'

'From your obvious indignation. But I'm afraid I can't discuss the matter.'

'I didn't come here to discuss it,' said the girl. 'I came here to tell you about it. That's quite a different thing. Now listen.'

The judge very deliberately looked at his paper. 'That's very childish. You're imprisoned with me here for the next half-hour. You might as well make the best of it. Or at least be grown up. You're behaving like I used to when I was twelve.'

After about half a minute the girl got up and came and sat next to the judge. He disregarded her. She edged closer. Now he had to do something about it.

'Kindly go back to your seat, madam.'

'That's better. You said something.'

'Kindly go back to your seat.'

'That's twice. Go on. Put me back. I shan't struggle – much. Why shouldn't I sit next to you?'

The judge got up and walked across to the corner seat in the farther part of the carriage and sat down. The girl waited a moment or two and then went over to him.

'Madam,' said the judge, 'if you don't stop annoying me, I shall pull the communication cord.'

'I shouldn't,' said the girl.

She looked at her knee which was showing slightly below her skirt.

'They mightn't believe me but it would be in all the papers. Wouldn't look so good. I shouldn't allege anything very terrible – just the sort of thing old gentlemen do –

your hand on my knee or something. But it would be an assault all the same. "Judge cleared of assault charge." Wouldn't look well, would it?'

The judge now had to do some extremely quick thinking. He was a highly intelligent man with a vivid imagination. If he pulled the communication cord and the guard arrived and she said that she had pulled it and made an allegation of a slight assault against him it would be a very serious matter for him. No Court, of course, could convict him upon that evidence but a good many people might think that it was true. It would have been much better for him if the allegation had been a wilder one. But people would ask themselves why she should make this very mild allegation that he simply put his hand upon her knee. And she was quite right in saying that old gentlemen did that sort of thing. He was still considering the matter when she spoke again.

'Look,' she said. 'I'll make a bargain with you. If you'll talk, I'll go and sit over the other side. How's that? Like this.'

She got up and went into the corner farther away from the judge, crossed her legs and twiddled her thumbs.

'Well, is it a bargain?'

The judge felt that he must not give in too far. That was the danger with blackmailers. What next might she ask?

'I warn you, madam, that, if you interfere with my comfort again, I'll pull the cord.'

'I only want to talk,' she said. 'But I shouldn't pull the cord. I don't want my name in the papers any more than you do. But, if it's got to be in, I'll have my money's worth. And you couldn't get me convicted of perjury either. You need two witnesses for that.'

She laughed. 'Fancy me telling a judge that.'

'You could be fined for interfering with my comfort,' said the judge. 'That's an offence.'

'That's a fine! I couldn't be sent to prison. Of course a poor woman wouldn't be able to pay the fine. Remember? And I'll tell you another thing. They might believe me not you. Everyone doesn't like judges the same as you do. So be sensible and talk. If you don't, *I* might pull it. And, if I just tell my modest little story – nothing flamboyant, no torn dresses – just "He leant forward and put his hand on my stockinged knee." My stockinged knee,' she repeated, and she put her hand on it. 'And you won't be able to raise the just-a-friendly-gesture defence because you'll have to say you never did it. So please talk. We haven't so long.'

'I will not discuss the case,' said the judge.

'That's better. Well, you can just listen. You behaved disgracefully at that trial. Not before the finding of guilty. I will say you were perfectly fair until then. But, when you let out that bit about the poor man, you were caught and you knew it. And you hadn't the courage or grace to admit it. But counsel had the courage all right and he wouldn't let go. And all you did at the end was to tell him to sit down. It was just abuse of power. Like post office clerks who won't attend to you or box office managers when the play's a success or anyone else who has a bit of power and abuses it. But you're a judge and you ought to know better.'

'Madam,' said the judge after some thought, 'your behaviour is intolerable. It probably amounts to contempt of Court and I expect I could have you sent to prison. Have *you* thought of that?'

It was the girl's turn to be shocked. But she was not going to show it more than she could help.

'Sent to prison?' she said. 'I couldn't be for talking to you here. And anyway I don't care. I've waited six weeks to say it and I will say it. You must be a small-minded man. You have so much power. There's no excuse for abusing it. There's much more excuse for the little people. Like me, I mean. I've just abused my power as a woman.'

'We can agree on that,' said the judge.

'But I was provoked. You weren't.'

'How were you provoked?' asked the judge.

'By your behaviour, of course.'

'It's you whose behaviour has been disgraceful, not mine, madam,' said the judge.

'I don't mean here,' said the girl. 'I mean at the trial.'

'Wives whose husbands fare badly in a Court of Law often blame the judge.'

'There was no excuse for refusing to listen any more.'

'There was every reason. Counsel just kept on repeating himself.'

'Only because you never dealt with his point about the poor man. Why did you talk about the poor man unless you had a fine in mind? "You can't buy your way out of this. A poor man couldn't pay a fine." What did that mean?'

The judge said nothing.

'Well, what did it mean?' she repeated. 'He asked you four times and I ask you once and you can't answer because you know there isn't an answer. Is there?'

'I don't propose to discuss the matter further with you, madam,' said the judge. 'If you choose to pull the communication cord, that is entirely a matter for you.'

He went back into his paper but he had no idea what he was supposed to be reading. He was thinking. Shortly before they arrived at the next station the judge suddenly spoke.

'Madam,' he said, 'as I said before, your behaviour has been intolerable. And, having had time to think about the matter, I am quite satisfied that you could be sent to prison for contempt of Court for talking to me in the way you have.'

'And I've had time to think about it too,' said the girl, 'and I don't care if you do. It'll only be one abuse of power followed by another.'

'Madam,' said the judge rather more gently, 'I didn't say that I was going to have you sent to prison. As a matter of fact, your criticism of my behaviour in Court was perfectly justified. And, when I next see the barrister in question, I shall apologise to him.'

'Come again?' said the girl.

'And in so far as you are concerned in the matter,' went on the judge, 'I apologise to you too. The sentence was fair. But I did not treat counsel fairly. And you are a very courageous young woman to have told me so.'

'Good gracious!' said the girl. 'I said you were a little man but my Lord, Sir, or whatever I should say, you're a big man. Thank you.'

The train drew in at the station and the judge got out as quickly as he could.

It was some time before he had the opportunity of seeing Arnold Blaize and apologising. At first he had intended to send for him at the earliest possible moment but then he realised that it was already six weeks after the trial and that would look rather odd. There was no reason why he should tell him about his extraordinary adventure in the train and, unless he gave some explanation, it would seem funny to wait for six weeks and then take the trouble to send for him to apologise. On the other hand, if he happened to meet him at some gathering, that was quite a different matter and he could take the opportunity of doing what he firmly intended to do ever since he had left the girl in the railway carriage.

The chance came at a garden party at one of the Inns of Court. He saw Blaize and went over to him. After a few general remarks he came to the point. Then he apologised handsomely and congratulated Blaize on the way he had stood up to him.

'That took a lot of courage,' he said.

The young man was embarrassed, but he eventually started to say: 'Oh, judge,' he began, 'it's – it's very good of – '

He broke off as he saw a girl coming towards them. 'Oh, judge,' he went on, 'might I introduce my wife?'

The girl in the train came up to them.

'Good gracious!' said the judge, and then he recovered himself and said quite naturally: 'How d'you do, Mrs Blaize?' They shook hands. 'Shall I tell him?' he asked. She begged him not to with her eyes.

'Tell me what, judge?' asked Blaize.

'But you must know already,' said the judge. The girl shook her head.

'Know what already?' asked Blaize.

'Well, if you don't, you should,' said the judge. 'And I propose to tell you.' He looked at the girl. 'You deserve it, you know,' he said. The girl still pleaded. There was a pause.

'Blaize,' went on the judge, 'I think you should know that you have a very attractive wife. It's time someone told you. She quite took my breath away.'

HENRY CECIL

ACCORDING TO THE EVIDENCE

Alec Morland is on trial for murder. He has tried to remedy the ineffectiveness of the law by taking matters into his own hands. Unfortunately for him, his alleged crime was not committed in immediate defence of others or of himself. In this fascinating murder trial you will not find out until the very end just how the law will interpret his actions. Will his defence be accepted or does a different fate await him?

THE ASKING PRICE

Ronald Holbrook is a fifty-seven-year-old bachelor who has lived in the same house for twenty years. Jane Doughty, the daughter of his next-door neighbours, is seventeen. She suddenly decides she is in love with Ronald and wants to marry him. Everyone is amused at first but then events take a disturbingly sinister turn and Ronald finds himself enmeshed in a potentially tragic situation.

'The secret of Mr Cecil's success lies in continuing to do superbly what everyone now knows he can do well.'
– *The Sunday Times*

HENRY CECIL

BRIEF TALES FROM THE BENCH

What does it feel like to be a Judge? Read these stories and you can almost feel you are looking at proceedings from the lofty position of the Bench.

With a collection of eccentric and amusing characters, Henry Cecil brings to life the trials in a County Court and exposes the complex and often contradictory workings of the English legal system.

'Immensely readable. His stories rely above all on one quality – an extraordinary, an arresting, a really staggering ingenuity.'
– *New Statesman*

BROTHERS IN LAW

Roger Thursby, aged twenty-four, is called to the bar. He is young, inexperienced and his love life is complicated. He blunders his way through a succession of comic adventures including his calamitous debut at the bar.

His career takes an upward turn when he is chosen to defend the caddish Alfred Green at the Old Bailey. In this first Roger Thursby novel Henry Cecil satirizes the legal profession with his usual wit and insight.

'Uproariously funny.' – *The Times*

'Full of charm and humour. I think it is the best Henry Cecil yet.' – P G Wodehouse

Henry Cecil

Hunt the Slipper

Harriet and Graham have been happily married for twenty years. One day Graham fails to return home and Harriet begins to realise she has been abandoned. This feeling is strengthened when she starts to receive monthly payments from an untraceable source. After five years on her own Harriet begins to see another man and divorces Graham on the grounds of his desertion. Then one evening Harriet returns home to find Graham sitting in a chair, casually reading a book. Her initial relief turns to anger and then to fear when she realises that if Graham's story is true, she may never trust his sanity again. This complex comedy thriller will grip your attention to the very last page.

Sober as a Judge

Roger Thursby, the hero of *Brothers in Law* and *Friends at Court*, continues his career as a High Court judge. He presides over a series of unusual cases, including a professional debtor and an action about a consignment of oranges which turned to juice before delivery. There is a delightful succession of eccentric witnesses as the reader views proceedings from the Bench.

'The author's gift for brilliant characterisation makes this a book that will delight lawyers and laymen as much as did its predecessors.' – *The Daily Telegraph*